On Her Own

**Center Point
Large Print**

**This Large Print Book carries the
Seal of Approval of N.A.V.H.**

On Her Own

Wanda E. Brunstetter

CENTER POINT PUBLISHING
THORNDIKE, MAINE

This Center Point Large Print edition
is published in the year 2008 by arrangement with
Barbour Publishing, Inc.

The text of this Large Print edition is unabridged. In other
aspects, this book may vary from the original edition.
Printed in the United States of America.
Set in 16-point Times New Roman type.

ISBN: 978-1-60285-137-5

Library of Congress Cataloging-in-Publication Data

Brunstetter, Wanda E.
    On her own / Wanda E. Brunstetter.--Center Point large print ed.
    p. cm.
    ISBN 978-1-60285-137-5 (lib. bdg. : alk. paper)
    1. Widows--Fiction. 2. Amish women--Fiction. 3. Amish--Fiction. 4. Webster
County (Mo.)--Fiction. 5. Large type books. I. Title.

PS3602.R864O6 2008
813'.6--dc22

2007039683

one

Cradling the infant she had given birth to a few moments ago, Barbara Zook lay exhausted against the damp pillow beneath her head.

"We have four sons now, David," she murmured into the stillness of her room. "I wish you were here to see your baby. I'm plannin' to name him after you." Unbidden tears sprang to her eyes as she struggled against the memory of what had happened eight months ago.

Barbara shuddered and closed her eyes. If she lived to be one hundred, she would never forget the life-changing afternoon when her whole world fell apart in one unsuspecting moment. Unwillingly, Barbara's mind drove her back to that Saturday afternoon when she was happy and secure in her marriage. When she had high hopes for the future.

Barbara sat in the rocking chair on the front porch of her Amish home, watching her three boys play in the yard, waiting for her husband's return. Today was their tenth wedding anniversary, and David had taken their horse and buggy to Seymour to pick up her gift. He'd said it was something special. Something Barbara wanted and needed.

She patted her stomach and smiled. *When David returns home, I'll give him my gift—the news that I'm pregnant again.* She'd known for a couple of weeks but wanted it to be a surprise. David would be so happy. Barbara was hopeful it would be a girl this time.

She planned to share her good news the moment David arrived, which she was sure would be soon. He'd been gone several hours already, and she couldn't imagine what could be keeping him.

It was almost time to start supper, and Barbara was on the verge of heading for the kitchen, when a police car pulled into her driveway. She stood on the porch as two uniformed men got out of the vehide and walked up to her.

Barbara's heart thudded in her chest. Something was wrong. She could feel it in every fiber of her being. "May I help you?' Her voice sounded strained even to her own ears.

"Mrs. Zook?"

Barbara nodded. "I'm David Zook's wife."

One of the men stepped closer. "I'm sorry to tell you this, but there's been an accident."

"Is it . . . David?"

"I'm afraid so. We were called to the scene by one of your English neighbors. They're the ones who iden-tified the deceased."

Deceased? The word echoed in Barbara's head like a woodpecker tapping on a tree. *It's not true. It can't be. David's alive. Today's our anniversary. He'll be home soon.*

"I'm sorry," the other officer said, "but a truck rear-ended your husband's buggy. The stove he had tied on the back flew forward and hit him in the head."

The porch swayed in an eerie sort of way, and Barbara gripped the railing tightly to keep from toppling over. *David's dead. He bought me a stove. David can't be dead. Today's our anniversary.*

The wail of an infant's cry sent Barbara's thoughts to the back of her mind. Her eyes burned with unshed tears as she forced herself to focus on the joy of having a new baby in her arms. Little David needed her, and so did her other three boys.

"I'll do whatever I need to in order to provide for my family," she murmured.

When a knock sounded at the bedroom door, Barbara called, "Come in."

The door creaked opened, and David's mother, Mavis, stuck her head through the opening. "How you doin'? About ready for some company? Your older boys would like to meet their new brother."

Barbara glanced down at her son, who was enjoying the first taste of his mother's milk. "Little David's eatin' at the moment." She smiled at her mother-in-law "You're welcome to come say hello to your new grandson, but let's wait 'til he's done nursing to introduce him to his big brothers, okay?"

"*Jah,* sure." Mavis entered the room and closed the door. "Alice told me it was another boy. Didn't know you'd named him David, though."

"Mom had already gone downstairs by the time I decided on a name. You're the first to hear."

As she moved closer to the bed, Mavis sniffed deeply, and her brown eyes filled with tears. "My son would be right proud to know he had a child named after him."

Barbara swallowed around the lump in her throat. "David never even knew I was pregnant. He died before I could share our surprise." She stared down at her infant son. "It breaks my heart to know this tiny fellow will never know his *daed*."

The wrinkles in Mavis's forehead became more pronounced. "If any of my sons were unmarried, I'd offer you one to marry . . . so's your boys wouldn't have to grow up without a father."

Barbara could hardly believe her mother-in-law had said such a thing. "We're not livin' by Old Testament customs, you know."

Mavis reached out to touch the baby's downy, dark head. "I realize that. But if I could do somethin' to help your situation, I surely would."

"You already have, Mavis. You and Jeremiah helped us aplenty, same as my folks have done."

Mavis nodded. "*Jah*. Your *mamm* has been good about watching your children so you can work in the harness shop."

Barbara thought about how determined David had been to open his own business here in Webster County, Missouri. Because of it, they had made enough money to put food on the table and pay the bills. And Barbara enjoyed working in the shop. To her, the smell of leather was like sweet perfume. Now the aroma reminded her of her beloved husband.

"This is a day of beginnings for David Zook Jr., and it's a day of endings for our friend Dan Hilty."

Mavis's statement jolted Barbara to the core. "Has somethin' happened to Dan?"

Her mother-in-law nodded soberly. "You didn't know?"

Barbara shook her head.

"I thought Alice might have told you before you went into labor."

"Mom never said anything. What happened?"

Mavis sat in the chair next to the bed. "He died of a heart attack early this mornin'."

"How terrible. I'm awful sorry for Margaret and her family." Barbara felt Dan's widow's pain as if it were her own. David had been gone eight months, but today it seemed as if she were living his death all over again. Giving birth to her husband's namesake was bitter-sweet, and hearing of someone else's loss was a reminder of her own suffering.

"Death comes to all," Mavis said in a hushed tone. "It was Dan's time to go."

Barbara had heard the bishop and others in their Amish community say the same thing many times whenever someone passed away. There were those who said that if the deceased person hadn't died one way, they would have another. "When your time's up, it's up," the bishop had told Barbara the day of David's funeral. She wasn't sure she accepted that concept. Accidents happened, true enough, but they were brought on because someone was careless or in the wrong place at the wrong time. If David hadn't gone to town the morning of their anniversary, he might be alive today.

Barbara saw no point in telling David's mother how she felt about things. She would probably end up arguing with her. "When's the funeral?" she asked.

"In a few days, I would think." Mavis patted Barbara's shoulder. "You'll not be expected to go, seein' as how you've just given birth and need to rest."

Barbara nodded. Rest. Yes, that's what she needed right now. She closed her eyes, feeling a desire for sleep overtake her. "Tell my boys they can see their little brother soon. After Davey and I have ourselves a little nap."

When Barbara heard a familiar *creak,* she knew Mavis had risen from the chair. The last thing she remembered was the bedroom door clicking shut.

Paul Hilty's hand shook as he reread the telegram that had been delivered a few moments ago to his cousin Abe's shop, where he worked. According to the message, Paul's oldest brother was dead.

Paul turned to face his cousin. "I've gotta go home. My brother passed away this morning."

Abe's dark eyebrows furrowed. "Which brother?"

"Dan. He had a heart attack."

"I'm sorry to hear that. He was helping your *daed* on the farm, isn't that right?"

Paul nodded. "Him, Monroe, and Elam. Now it'll

just be Pop and my two younger brothers." He grimaced. "No doubt my *daed* will be after me to come back to Missouri so I can help 'em work in the fields."

"You'll be leaving Pennsylvania, then?"

"Not if I can help it." Paul swallowed hard. "I will need to go back for the funeral, though."

"I'd close the shop and go with you, but I just got in several new orders, and I'd get really behind if we were both gone. The man I recently hired is too new. I can't expect him to know what to do in my absence."

Paul shook his head. "That's okay. You're needed here. I'm sure the folks will understand."

The bus ride to Missouri gave Paul plenty of time to think. What kind of reception would he receive from his family in Webster County? How long would he be expected to stay after the funeral?

Paul thought about that day four years ago when he decided to leave home. He'd been farming with his dad and brothers ever since he finished the eighth grade—first when they lived in Pennsylvania, where Paul had been born, and later, when Pop moved his family to Missouri. Paul had never enjoyed farming. He wanted to learn a trade—preferably harness making. But there was already one harness shop in the area, owned by David Zook. Paul didn't figure there was a need in their small community for another one, and he was sure David wouldn't hire him, since his wife worked there with him.

When his cousin Abe, who had a harness shop in

Lancaster County, Pennsylvania, invited Paul to come work for him, Paul jumped at the chance. Paul's mother said she didn't understand why he was leaving, and his dad blew up and shouted at Paul, calling him a stubborn fool.

It was for the best, Paul thought as he gripped the armrest of his seat on the bus. *I'm much happier living in Pennsylvania than I was in Missouri.*

A twinge of guilt stabbed his conscience like a needle prick. Truth was, he did like his work at Abe's harness shop, but he wasn't really happy. Abe kept telling Paul he needed to find a good wife and have a passel of *kinner,* then he'd know what true happiness was.

Abe had been married to Carolyn for five years, and they had three children already He often said how much joy he found in being a husband and father.

Paul didn't think he would ever get married. He was thirty years old and had never had a serious relationship with a woman. He shied away from women because he thought he wouldn't make a good father and therefore wouldn't be a good husband.

Paul thought about his brother's untimely death. Dan's passing was only eight months after David Zook had been killed. Mom had written to Paul and told him that a truck had hit David's buggy, leaving his wife to raise their three sons and manage the harness shop alone.

I wonder how Barbara's been doing. He also wondered if she'd hired someone to help in the shop.

Paul stared out the bus window, barely noticing the

passing scenery. *Don't get any dumb ideas. You're coming back to Pennsylvania as soon as Dan's funeral is over.*

two

"There's no reason for you to stay here with me," Barbara said to her mother, who stood inside the kitchen doorway. "You and Dad should both go to the funeral."

Mom clicked her tongue. "And leave you here in a weakened condition with three little ones and a new *boppli?* Never!"

Barbara knew there was no arguing with her mother once she'd made up her mind about something. She pushed a wayward strand of hair from her face and grimaced. She hadn't done a good job of putting up her bun this morning. For that matter, she didn't feel like she had done much of anything right since she got out of bed. She'd yelled at Joseph and Zachary for being too loud, scolded Aaron for picking on his younger brothers, and dropped a carton of eggs in the middle of the kitchen floor. Maybe it was because of her "weakened condition." Or perhaps it was the fact that Dan Hilty's death had opened up the wounds of losing her husband, making her irritable. In either case, Barbara knew she could not go to the funeral that morning.

She moved to the table and took a seat. "You're right, Mom. I do need some help today. Would you be willing to watch the boys while I tend to the *boppli?*" She was glad her folks lived next door. At least the children would be near enough for Barbara to have lunch with them. She didn't want her boys to think she had abandoned them now that there was a baby brother in the house.

Mom sat in the chair opposite Barbara and poured them both a cup of tea from the pot sitting in the center of the table. "I'd be happy to look out for your brood." She handed a cup to Barbara. "Your *daed*'s got the boys out helpin' with chores. After breakfast is over, I'll take 'em over to my place and find somethin' to keep everyone occupied so you can rest awhile. You look all done in."

Barbara drew in a deep breath and released it with a groan. "Sure will be glad when little David starts sleepin' more and eatin' less often. He woke me every couple hours last night."

Her mother nodded, and her blue eyes held a note of sympathy. "All the more reason you should rest during the day whenever possible."

The wooden chair groaned as Barbara leaned against the back. "It's not just the lack of sleep that has me feelin' so down."

"What else is botherin' you?"

"I'm worried about the harness shop. I appreciate that Dad's been helpin' me since David died, but he can't run it alone. His arthritic fingers don't work so good, and there's too much to be done for just one man."

Mom tapped her fingernails along the edge of the table. "Maybe you could hire someone to help while you're gettin' your strength back."

"Who would I hire? No one in our community does harness work, and Dad doesn't know enough about it to teach them." Barbara sniffed. "Truth is, Dad barely manages when I'm not there to oversee things."

"That's true. Maybe keepin' the shop isn't such a good idea." Mom leaned slightly forward. "Have you thought about runnin' an ad in the *Budget* to try and sell off the supplies?"

"I could never part with David's harness shop. It meant too much to him." Barbara stared down at the table. "And it means a lot to me, too. I enjoy working there, Mom. Can you understand that?"

"What I understand is that my daughter's been workin' hard in that shop, even throughout most of her pregnancy." Mom sighed. "I know you want to prove you can support yourself and the boys, but you can't do it alone. Your *daed* will help in the shop as long as he's able, and I'm sure David's folks will help with finances if needed."

Barbara pushed her chair back and stood. "I won't have you and Dad, or my husband's parents, taking care of us until the boys are all raised. That's my job, and I'll do it." She started for the door leading to the upstairs but turned back around. "I hope you know that I appreciate your concerns and all the help you've offered."

Mom nodded. "I know."

"I'm goin' upstairs to check on the *boppli,* but I'll be back before Dad and the *kinner* come in for breakfast."

Barbara was almost to the kitchen door when her mother said, "Say, I just thought of somethin'."

"What's that?"

"I spoke with Faith Hertzler yesterday morning, and she said she'd seen Dan's brother Paul. Guess he came home for the funeral."

Barbara faced her mother. "*Jah,* I suppose he would."

"Paul's been working in Pennsylvania these last four years . . . working at a harness shop."

"So I heard."

"Maybe Paul would be willin' to stick around awhile and work at your shop. Want me to have your *daed* talk to him about it today?"

Barbara shook her head. "Not at his brother's funeral."

"How about tomorrow, then?"

"Maybe. Let me think on it awhile."

"Sounds *gut* to me. You think, and I'll be prayin'."

Barbara smiled at her mother's exuberance. "I'll pray, too, Mom. Just like I always do when I have a big decision to make."

Paul left the confines of his folks' house, full of people who had come to the meal following Dan's funeral. Some were milling about the living room while others stood outside on the lawn, visiting and offering their condolences to Dan's widow and the rest of the Hilty family.

Paul felt as out of place as a bullfrog in a chicken coop. Mom, his sisters Rebekah and Susan, and his brothers Monroe and Elam had been friendly enough. Pop was a different story, though. He'd been cold as a block of ice toward Paul ever since he arrived home last night. It wasn't fair. Shouldn't Paul have the right to work at the trade of his choice? Why should Pop expect all of his sons to be farmers just because he had chosen to be one?

Paul hurried past the tables, where many of the older people sat visiting, and headed for the barn. He had to be by himself for a while. He needed time to think. Time to breathe.

As soon as he opened the barn door, the familiar aroma of sweaty horses, sweet-smelling hay, and fresh manure assaulted Paul's senses. His ears perked up at the gentle sound of a horse's whinny, and his eyes feasted on the place where he and his siblings used to play.

Paul glanced at the wooden rafters. The rope swing was still there, hanging from the beam overhead. So many times his brothers had argued over who would get the first turn on the swing that transported them from the hayloft to the pile of straw where they dropped at will. Not Paul, though. He was afraid of heights and had no desire to dangle from any rope suspended so high.

Paul moved away from the old swing. He was about

to enter one of the horses' stalls when he heard the barn door open and shut. He whirled around.

"Hope I didn't startle you." Noah Hertzler stood there, holding his black felt hat in his hands. "I saw you come inside and wanted to offer my condolences on the loss of your brother. Dan will surely be missed, and I'm real sorry about his passing."

Paul reached out to shake Noah's hand. "*Danki.* I appreciate your kind words."

"How have you been?" Noah asked.

"I was doing good 'til I got the news that my brother died."

Noah nodded. "I understand. My *mamm* passed on a year ago. I still miss her a lot."

Paul swallowed hard. "It's never easy to lose a loved one."

"No, it's not. Do you like Pennsylvania? Has it changed much?" Noah asked.

"I like it well enough. But the Lancaster area is a lot more crowded than when I was growing up there." Paul shrugged. "I put up with all the tourists so I can do what I like best."

"You mean harness making and repairing?"

Paul nodded. "Abe also sells and fixes leather shoes and boots."

"I'm sure you must've heard about David Zook passing on," Noah said.

"*Jah.* Such a shame. How's his wife faring? Does she have anyone to help her in the harness shop?"

Noah shook his head. "Just her *daed,* and his fingers

don't work so good, what with his arthritis and all."

"So it's just Barbara and Samuel?"

"Right now it's only him. Barbara won't be back to work 'til her strength returns and the *new boppli*'s a bit bigger."

Paul's mouth dropped open. "She's got another child? Mom never mentioned that in any of her letters."

Noah took a seat on a bale of straw, and Paul did the same. "Barbara gave birth to son number four the same day your brother died. David never even knew she was in a family way." Noah slowly shook his head. "Faith told me Barbara's real tired. That's why she's not here today."

"Wouldn't expect her to be under the circumstances."

Noah cleared his throat. "I . . . uh . . . was wondering if you might want to stick around awhile. Maybe see about working at Zook's Harness Shop."

Paul felt a rush of adrenaline course through his body. Why couldn't that opportunity have been there four years ago? "If I did offer my services, it would only be until Barbara gets back on her feet again."

"Does that mean you'd never consider staying in Webster County?"

Paul shook his head. "Only came home for Dan's funeral. Figured I might stay a week or so to visit family and friends. My sisters live in Jamesport now, and they'll only be here a week, too."

Noah's expression seemed sincere, and his dark eyes were full of understanding. "Before Faith and I were married, she came home not planning to stay, either."

Paul opened his mouth to say something, but Noah cut him off. "After a time, Faith realized her home was here, and she knew she was supposed to stay." He smiled. "Of course, marrying me was part of the deal."

"Faith didn't have a father who wanted her to do something she didn't want to do," Paul mumbled. "My *daed* wants me to farm, and if I stick around too long, he'll start pressing me on the issue."

Noah stood and arched his back. "Faith was away from home for ten years. She was telling jokes and yodeling in the English world."

"I remember."

"She and her *daed* didn't see eye to eye on her yodeling, but he's come to terms with it now." Noah chuckled. "Of course, she don't normally yodel in front of him."

Paul stood, too. "Even if Pop and I could mend our fences, I still wouldn't stay here."

"Why not?"

"I like working on harnesses; and there ain't room for two shops in our community that would be doing the same thing."

Noah thumped Paul on the back. "You could work for Barbara indefinitely."

Paul's face heated up. He wasn't about to spend the rest of his life working for Barbara Zook. In his mind, she shouldn't even be running the harness shop. That was men's work, plain and simple.

"I won't be staying in Webster County." Paul moved toward the door, and Noah followed. "I will drop by and see Barbara, though. I need to offer my condolences on the loss of her husband."

three

Barbara was napping on the sofa when a knock at the back door wakened her. Figuring it to be her mother, she called, "Come in!" She had just swung her legs over the couch when she heard the door open.

"I'm in the living room, Mom!" she called.

A few seconds later, a tall, blond man entered the room. He wore the traditional Amish garb: a straw hat, short-sleeved cotton shirt, and dark trousers held up by tan suspenders. "I'm not your *mamm,* but you did invite me to come in," he said in a sheepish voice.

Barbara's mouth hung open, and she knew she probably looked like a wrinkled mess. She'd reclined on the couch for a short rest and ended up falling into a deep sleep. The baby was sleeping in his crib upstairs, and the boys were next door at her folks' place. It had been the perfect time to rest. The last thing Barbara expected when she woke up was to see a man standing in her living room.

"Paul Hilty?"

"*Jah,* it's me." He shifted his long legs and shuffled his black boots against the hardwood floor. "Sorry if I startled you."

Barbara's hand went instinctively to her hair, as she

checked to be sure her *kapp* was in place. "No, no, that's okay. I mean—it's *gut* to see you."

"And you, as well." When Paul smiled, his face turned a light shade of pink. "You're lookin' good these days."

Barbara felt her cheeks grow warm as she stood. "Sorry I couldn't make it to the funeral yesterday. I had a baby a few days ago and haven't gotten my strength back yet."

A look of concern clouded Paul's deeply set blue eyes. "*Jah,* I heard that. Also heard about David's death. I came by to tell you how sorry I am."

Barbara sank back to the couch. "It's been a rough eight months."

Paul removed his hat and took a couple of steps forward. "I can only imagine."

She swallowed around the lump in her throat. It was hard not to feel sorry for herself, especially with Paul standing there, offering sympathy. "Have a seat," she said, remembering her manners.

He seated himself in the rocker close to the sofa, looking more uncomfortable by the minute. Barbara had not known Paul when they were children, as his parents had moved here to Missouri when he was a teenager. Paul helped his dad farm for a while, but then he'd been invited to work in his cousin's harness shop in Lancaster County, so he'd moved back to Pennsylvania. She'd heard it was against his dad's wishes, but she couldn't fault Paul for wanting to work where he felt most comfortable. She would do most anything to keep working in David's harness shop.

Only the soft ticking of the mantel clock broke the quiet in the room. Barbara sat there with her hands folded in her lap. Paul moved slowly back and forth in the rocker.

Finally, she spoke again. "How have you been? Are you happy livin' in Lancaster County?"

He stopped rocking and sat straight as a board. "I like working on harnesses, but Lancaster's a bit overcrowded for my taste."

She was tempted to ask why he stayed, but she figured it probably had to do with the job he enjoyed. "I can imagine. I hear there's plenty of English livin' in that area, and tourists come by the thousands to get a look at the Plain folks there."

Paul nodded. "Not like here, where so few tourists know about us."

"They probably wouldn't care anyway, seein' as how we're such a small community."

"Guess you're right about that."

"How long will you be stayin' in Webster County?" she asked.

He twisted the edge of his straw hat in his hands. "Guess that all depends."

"On what?"

"I had only intended on staying a few days, a week at the most. I could stay longer if there was a need, though."

"You mean if your *daed* needed you to help farm?"

He shook his head. "No way! I gave up farming when I moved from Webster County, and I ain't about to go back to it again."

"I see."

Paul rubbed the bridge of his nose and leaned slightly forward. "The thing is . . . I was wondering if you might be needing someone to run the harness shop since David's gone and you're not able to work right now."

She drew in a deep breath as she thought about the passage of scripture she'd read the night before: Ecclesiastes 4:9-10. *"Two are better than one; because they have a good reward for their labour. For if they fall, the one will lift up his fellow: but woe to him that is alone when he falleth; for he hath not another to help him up."*

"Actually, I could use some help," she admitted reluctantly. "Dad's working there, of course, but his fingers won't let him do a lot, and it's gonna be a few more weeks before I can return to work."

"That's what I figured."

"What about your other job? Can your cousin get by without your help for a few weeks?"

He shrugged. "Don't see why not. He just hired on another man. Unless things get busier than they have been, I'm sure Abe won't mind if I stay here awhile and help in David's shop."

"It's my shop now," Barbara corrected. She didn't know why she felt the need to clarify that.

"Right. I understand, and I—"

The sound of her baby's cry halted Paul's words.

Barbara jumped up. "That's little David. I should go tend to him."

Paul stood. "Of course. I can come back some other time."

She waved her hand. "That's okay. Why don't you make yourself comfortable while I tend to the *boppli?* When I'm done, we can talk more about your workin' in the harness shop."

He sat down again. "Sounds fine to me."

Barbara started for the stairs but turned back. "Help yourself to a cup of coffee. I think there's still some in the pot on the stove." She left the room before he had a chance to respond, glad for the opportunity to think more about Paul's offer.

Paul remained in his chair for several minutes after Barbara went upstairs. The baby's crying had stopped, so he figured she must have things under control.

Paul couldn't believe how much Barbara had changed since he'd seen her four years ago. She used to be kind of plump, but now she was almost too thin. Had the years of working in the harness shop taken their toll on her, or had she lost the weight after David died? He'd heard of people nearly starving themselves to death when a mate had been taken, but Barbara was a new mother. Seemed like she should weigh a lot more than she did.

One more reason I need to stick around and help out, he mused. *She probably doesn't eat right because she worries about the harness shop and how she'll provide for her family.*

Paul got to his feet and moved to the unlit fireplace. It was late spring. Getting too warm for any fires right now.

Barbara's a fine-looking woman. Funny I never paid much attention to her before. He slapped the side of his head, as though the action might get him thinking straight again. Of course he wouldn't have been eyeing Barbara before. She was married to David Zook, and it wouldn't have been right for him to pay special attention to some other man's wife. David and Barbara were already courting by the time Paul and his family moved to Webster County so Pop could farm in an area where the English wouldn't crowd him out. Even if Paul had noticed Barbara when she was still a Raber, it wouldn't have done him any good. She'd been David's girl from the very beginning. Besides, she was two years older than Paul and probably wouldn't have given him a second look during their teen years.

Might as well get myself a cup of coffee, he mused. *Leastways it'll give me something to do 'til she gets back, and hopefully it will keep me from all this crazy thinking.*

In the kitchen, Paul found a pot of coffee warming on the propane stove. He located a man-sized mug in one of the cupboards and had just poured himself some coffee when the back door swung open.

When he turned around, a young boy stood there.

26

He had brunette hair like Barbara's, and his eyes, also dark, were huge as flapjacks.

"Who are you, and what are ya doin' with my pa's coffee mug?" The child took one step forward and planted his hands on his hips.

"I'm Paul Hilty," Paul said, extending his free hand. "You must be one of Barbara's boys."

The lad thrust out his chin and pushed back his shoulders, but he didn't reach for Paul's hand. "My name's Aaron. I'm her oldest son."

Paul opened his mouth to reply, but Aaron cut him off. "When I grow up, I plan to take over Pa's harness shop." He stared down at Paul's black boots. "My mom'll be old by then and probably won't wanna work on harnesses no more."

When Paul chuckled, Aaron scowled at him. "What's so funny?"

"Nothing. I mean, it tickles me the way you talk of your mom getting old and you taking her place in the shop."

"I don't think it's funny a'tall."

Paul took a sip of coffee and motioned toward the table. "Let's have a seat and we can get better acquainted." He pulled out a chair and sat down, but the boy stood there as though glued to the spot.

"Ya still haven't said why you're usin' my *daed*'s mug."

Paul eyed the cup in question, then nodded toward the empty chair to his left. "Sit down, and I'll tell you."

Aaron took a seat, but he wasn't smiling.

"I came over to visit with your mother, and then the *boppli* started fussing, so Barbara—I mean, your *mamm*—said I should help myself to some coffee while she took care of your little brother."

"But ya shouldn't be usin' Pa's cup," the child persisted.

Paul was tempted to remind Aaron that his pa was dead and it shouldn't matter who drank from his cup, but he thought better of it. No use getting the boy riled, especially if Barbara decided to hire Paul in the harness shop. Aaron undoubtedly still missed his father. The idea of someone using his mug could be a powerful reminder of the boy's loss.

Paul stood and poured the coffee into another cup; then he set David's mug in the kitchen sink. "Better?" he asked as he returned to his seat.

The boy only nodded in reply.

"How old are you, Aaron?"

"Almost nine."

"Hmm. Won't be long until you can begin helping your *mamm* in the shop."

The child shrugged. "Used to help my *daed* some, when I wasn't in school."

"What grade are you in?" Paul asked.

"Second."

"You have seven more years, then."

"Yep."

Paul took another swig of coffee, wishing Barbara would return so he'd have another adult to talk to.

"Want some cookies to dunk in your coffee?"

Aaron's question took Paul by surprise, and he jumped.

"What's the matter? Ya got a fly on your nose?"

"Huh?"

"You're kind of jumpy, wouldn't ya say?"

Paul cleared his throat. "I'm fine. Just a bit restless is all."

"Some cookies might help."

Paul studied the boy's round face. Paul was pretty sure the subject of cookies had come up because Aaron wanted some, not because the child thought Paul needed something to dunk in his coffee.

"You're right. Cookies would be nice." Paul grinned. "You know where there might be some?"

Aaron jumped up and dashed across the room. He returned a few seconds later with a yellow ceramic jar. "Chocolate chip." He set the container on the table and headed for the refrigerator. "Think I'll have me some milk so's I can dunk, too."

Paul thought about how he had enjoyed cookies and cold goat's milk as a boy. Peanut butter with raisins had been his favorite, and Mom made them often. He watched Aaron fill a tall glass with milk, dip his cookie up and down a couple of times, then chomp it down in two bites.

"This is sure *gut*. Grandma made these just for me."

"Your grandparents live next door, isn't that right?"

Aaron grabbed another cookie. "Yep. Grandpa and

Grandma Raber keep an eye on me and my brothers durin' the day. Grandma and Grandpa Zook live a couple miles down the road."

"Does your grandma know where you are right now?" Paul questioned.

"Of course. Told her I was comin' over here to see if Mama needed me for anythin'." Aaron licked a glob of chocolate off his fingertips. "Sure never expected to find a stranger sittin' in our kitchen, though."

"I'm not really a stranger," Paul said. "I used to live in Webster County. I've known your folks for some time."

"It's your brother who died last week, ain't it?"

"*Jah,* my brother Dan. His funeral was yesterday."

"When ya said your last name, I put two and two together."

Paul grinned. *Not only feisty, but a right smart little fellow.*

"What'd ya come over to see Mama about?"

"He's comin' to work for me startin' Saturday."

Paul turned his head. He hadn't realized Barbara had entered the room. She held a baby in her arms, and her face was slightly flushed. He also noticed that she'd changed from the brown dress she'd had on earlier and was now wearing a gray dress with a dark blue cape and apron. *She looks like an angel,* he thought. *An angel with four children!*

four

Paul was about to enter Zook's Harness Shop, but he slowed his pace, still unsure he'd made the right decision in agreeing to come to work here. *Maybe it won't be so bad,* he decided. *Barbara did say she would be staying at the house to do paperwork and tend to her children.* He figured he would pretty much be in charge of things since Samuel Raber had arthritis and, according to Barbara, didn't know a great deal about the business of harness making and repairing.

As he opened the door and stepped into the shop, Paul drew in a deep breath. The smell of raw leather, linseed oil, and pungent dye hung in the air. He glanced around. Several harnesses and bridles were looped from ceiling hooks. Enormous sheets of leather, rolled loosely like oversized cinnamon sticks, poured out of shelves along one side of the shop. He noticed hundreds of snaps, rings, buckles, and rivets nestled in open boxes lined neatly along one wooden shelf. Piled on the cement floor were bits of leather scraps, resembling spaghetti noodles. It was a comfortable feeling to be inside the harness shop. He'd only been gone from his cousin's place a few days, and already he missed it.

Paul saw no sign of Samuel, so he headed toward the back of the building. Two oversized sewing machines, run by an air compressor, sat side by side on a heavy table. A row of tools spilled out of round wooden holders on the wide workbench nearby. "Hello," he called. "Anybody here?"

Barbara's dad stepped out of the back room. Paul observed the man's slight limp as he headed toward him.

"Paul Hilty, it's nice to see ya again." Samuel extended his hand, and Paul couldn't help but notice the red, arthritic fingers.

"Nice to see you, as well." He cleared his throat. "I . . . uh . . . assume Barbara told you I'd be working here awhile."

Samuel smiled through the reddish beard that matched his bangs, which were cropped straight across his forehead. The sides of the man's auburn hair were streaked with gray. "It'll be *gut* to have ya helpin'." Samuel held up his hands. "These fingers don't work so good no more. And to tell ya the truth, when Barbara's not here to show me what to do, I often flounder."

Paul nodded. "I'll do whatever I can to help."

Samuel made a sweeping gesture. "Assemblin' a harness can be complicated. It involves dozens of snaps, straps, and buckles, all connected in a particular way." He grinned, and his cheeks flamed. "Guess ya already know that, what with ya workin' at a harness shop in Pennsylvania and all."

"*Jah,* I've been working for my cousin Abe."

"You like it there better'n here?"

Paul shrugged. "It's okay. But the area has sure gotten crowded over the last several years."

Samuel frowned. "I'd never want to live anyplace

but Webster County, Missouri. Nothin' like the quiet, peaceful life, that's what I say."

"So what jobs are needing to be done right now?" Paul asked.

Samuel motioned toward the desk near the front door. "There's a folder with all the job orders, and I'm way behind."

Paul rolled up his cotton shirtsleeves, eager to get busy. "I'll take a look-see."

Barbara glanced at the battery-operated clock above the refrigerator and poured herself a cup of tea. It was eight fifteen, and she'd sent the boys over to her mother's. She hadn't slept well last night, as the baby had been fussy and demanded several feedings. She wished she could go back to bed, but she had some bills that needed paying and paperwork for the business to get done.

She yawned and moved to the window. An open buggy sat next to the harness shop. She figured it must be Paul's. Most of their customers didn't show up until nine or after.

Barbara felt a sense of relief knowing her dad would have help in the shop now, but a part of her bristled at the thought of anyone taking her place. She loved working with leather and missed it terribly.

"I need to eat enough, rest more, and get my strength back so I can work in the shop again," she murmured as she took a seat at the table. "Then Paul will be free to return to Pennsylvania."

Barbara's hand trembled as she set her cup down. She'd been much weaker since Davey's birth than she had been when her other three boys were born. Maybe she'd done too much during her pregnancy. Mom sure thought that was the case and had said so several times. Perhaps she had lost more blood with this delivery, and that had left her feeling tired. Or maybe she was emotionally drained, having had to go through the ordeal without her husband by her side.

She leaned forward and rubbed her temples, trying to keep the threatening tears at bay. Feeling sorry for herself wouldn't help a thing. She pushed away from the table and stood. "What I need to do is go upstairs and check on the *boppli,* then get busy with those bills."

Paul stood at the workbench, focused on the job at hand. Connecting the breast strap of a harness to a huge three-way snap required some fancy looping. His hand wove in and out, neatly tacking the strap at the end.

"That's some fine work," Samuel. said as he peered over Paul's shoulder. "It's clear ya know exactly what you're doin'."

Paul shrugged. "Took me awhile to get the hang of it when I first started learning, but I've done this type of thing many times already."

Samuel stepped over a pile of dirty leather straps and buckles. "Always got lots of harnesses people bring in to get cleaned and repaired." He grunted. "If they'd take better care of 'em, they'd pretty well last forever."

"You're right about that," Paul agreed. "Folks need to bring their harnesses in for cleaning and oiling at least once a year, but many don't."

Samuel bent down and picked up a leather strap. "With my arthritic hands, cleanin' things like this is about the only thing I do well out here in the shop."

Before Paul could respond, the older man continued. "I put the dirty ones in a tub of warm water with saddle soap, then scrub 'em real good."

Paul was about to comment again, only this time he was interrupted when a truck rumbled into the yard and pulled up in front of the shop. A middle-aged English man ambled in, lugging a worn-out saddle, which he promptly dropped on the floor. "Need to have this gone over. Can you do that for me, Sam?"

"If it's just a good cleanin' you're after, I can manage it fine. But if the saddle needs a lot of fixin', then here's your man." Samuel motioned toward Paul. "Paul Hilty, meet Frank Henderson. He lives near Springfield."

"It's nice to meet you," Paul said, extending his hand.

"Howdy." As Frank returned the handshake, he looked a bit perplexed. "Where's Barbara? Isn't she working here anymore?"

"My daughter had a baby a few days ago, so she's takin' some time away from the shop. Paul's from Pennsylvania. He came here for his brother's funeral, and he's agreed to help out 'till she's able to handle things again."

Paul squatted down and studied the worn-looking saddle. It needed more than soap and water, but he was sure it could be salvaged. "We'll give it a good going-over." He looked up at Samuel. "You want to write up the work order, or should I?"

Samuel shrugged. "Makes no never mind to me. Until Barbara returns, you're the boss."

Paul thought about Barbara and how pale and thin she appeared. A *woman like her ought to just be caring for her* kinner, *not trying to run a business—especially one that often requires heavy lifting.*

"Why don't you write up the order?" Paul suggested. "I'll get back to work on that breast strap." He nodded at Frank. "Nice to meet you. We'll drop a card in the mail when your saddle's done."

"Appreciate that."

Paul turned back to his job.

Two more customers showed up during the morning hours, both English men. Paul took time out to meet them and see what they needed, but he left the paperwork up to Barbara's dad.

He was surprised when Samuel touched his shoulder and said, "Aaron just popped by to say food's on the table. Ya comin' up to the house for the noon meal?"

Paul had been so caught up in his work he hadn't realized it was lunchtime. "How come the boy's home from school today?"

"It's Saturday. No school 'til Monday, and then only

another few weeks until the *kinner* will be out for the summer."

"Oh." Paul had been out of school for so long, he'd forgotten the summer break began in early May.

"So you comin' up to the house or not?"

"I . . . uh . . . brought my lunch pail along. Figured I'd eat out here."

Samuel shook his head. "No way. You been workin' hard all mornin' and need a hot meal: Alice has probably got a place set for ya at the table, and believe me, you don't wanna disappoint that wife of mine."

Paul scratched the side of his head. "Well, I—"

"Barbara and the boys will be joinin' us, and I'm sure she'd like to hear how your first day on the job has been goin'."

"Guess I'd better say yes then."

Samuel grinned. "Glad to hear it."

"How come such a big meal today?" Barbara asked when she entered her mother's kitchen and saw all the food sitting out.

Mom placed a platter of ham in the center of the table and smiled. "I figured your *daed* would be bringin' Paul Hilty up to the house for lunch, and I know how hungry these men can be after workin' all mornin'."

An image of David popped into Barbara's head. She remembered him saying many times that the noon meal needed to be the heartiest of the day. *"Fuels the body after workin' all mornin' and gives one strength for the afternoon,"* he used to say.

Barbara's mother touched her arm. "You still look tired. Didn't you get a nap this mornin'?"

"Every time I laid down, Davey started to fuss. Now the little fellow's fast asleep in the crib in your spare bedroom."

Mom clucked her tongue. "Isn't that the way? All durin' her babyhood, your sister Clara was always wide awake when she should have been sleepin'."

Barbara chuckled. "You had five daughters with completely different personalities to raise, and I've been blessed with four boys who are equally different." She moved across the room toward the propane stove. "What can I do to help with the meal?"

Mom shook her head. "Everything's just about ready, so sit yourself down and relax 'til the men and boys come inside."

"Speakin' of the boys, where are my other three this afternoon? Haven't seen nor heard from them all mornin'."

"A few minutes ago I sent Aaron out to the harness shop to tell the menfolk lunch was ready. The two younger ones have been playin' on the back porch for the last hour or so."

Barbara pulled out a chair and sat down. "Sure hope Aaron does what you asked. He used to help his *daed* with little things in the shop, whenever he wasn't in school, but since David's death, he seems to have lost interest." She sighed. "Now I can barely get him to go in the shop at all."

Mom placed a bowl of coleslaw on the table. "The boy probably misses his *daed,* and bein' in the shop is a reminder that David's gone."

"Maybe so." Tears sprang to Barbara's eyes. "Aaron reminds me of David in so many ways. He enjoys workin' with his hands, same as his *daed* did."

"Maybe someday, when you're ready to give up the shop, he'll take it over."

Barbara nodded. "Might could be. He's not old enough to do a whole lot out there yet, but after he's done with school and is ready to learn a trade, we'll see if he has any interest in the harness business."

Her mother smiled. "If he takes after his *mamm,* he surely will."

five

When Paul entered the Rabers' kitchen, the first person he saw was Barbara. She sat at the table, holding her baby. He halted inside the door and stared. The sight of her kissing the infant's downy, dark head brought a lump to his throat. He'd seen plenty of women with babies, but never had it affected him like this.

What's the matter with me? Maybe I worked too hard this morning and it addled my brain.

"Hello, Paul," Barbara said. "How'd it go this morning?"

He stepped forward and hung his straw hat on the closest wall peg. "Everything went fine. There's a lot to be done, that's for sure."

She nodded. "With me not being able to work for the few weeks before the baby came, we really got behind."

"We'll catch up quick with this man mindin' the shop," Samuel said, following Paul into the kitchen. "I've never seen anyone work as hard as him."

Paul's ears burned, and he reached up to rub them, hoping to hide his embarrassment.

"I–I'm glad to hear it." Barbara's voice wavered when she spoke.

Alice Raber lumbered across the room, her generous frame pushing at the seams of her long blue dress. "If you men have already washed, then sit yourselves down at the table, and I'll call the boys."

"We cleaned up at the utility sink in the harness shop," Samuel said, "so we're ready to eat."

"I'll be right back," his wife said, and she went out the door. Samuel pulled out the chair at the head of the table and sat down, then motioned for Paul to do the same.

Paul took a seat but shifted uncomfortably in his chair. He felt out of place and wished he had stayed at the shop to eat lunch.

Barbara seemed equally ill at ease. She kept her attention on the baby more than anywhere else.

The tantalizing aroma of sugar-cured ham tickled Paul's nose and made his stomach rumble. This meal was bound to taste better than the cold sandwich and apple he'd brought to work with him that morning.

Struggling to come up with something intelligent to say, Paul felt relief when Alice returned to the kitchen with three young boys in tow.

"Paul, these are Barbara's boys," she said, tapping each one on the shoulder. "This is Aaron—he's close to nine. Joseph's nearly six, and Zachary is three and a half."

Paul nodded as the boys took their seats. "I met Aaron the other day. It's nice to meet the rest of you."

The two younger ones giggled, and Joseph nudged Aaron. Paul didn't know what they found so amusing and wondered if they might be laughing at him.

As soon as Alice sat down, Samuel cleared his throat and everyone bowed their heads for silent prayer. When Samuel cleared his throat a second time, Paul knew it was time to eat.

"Why don't you give me the *boppli,* and I'll put him in the crib?" Barbara's mother suggested. "That way you'll have both hands free to eat."

"I'm good at doing things with one hand," Barbara replied. She glanced at Paul and caught him staring at her. *Does he think I'm overly protective?* She looked away and reached for her glass of water.

"You're not gonna let me put the *boppli* down?" Mom persisted.

Barbara lifted the infant and placed him across her shoulder. "He's fine, and so am I."

Her mother shrugged but made no reply.

Barbara speared a piece of ham with her fork and realized as soon as it touched her plate that it would be difficult to cut with only one hand. Little David was almost asleep; she could feel the warmth of his head against her neck and hear his even breathing. A weary sigh escaped her lips. "Maybe I will put him down."

She sensed Paul's eyes upon her as she stood and slipped out of the room.

When she returned a few minutes later, Dad and Paul were engaged in conversation, while Mom looked content overseeing the boys. Barbara lingered in the kitchen doorway, watching the scene. Everyone seemed to be enjoying their meal and the camaraderie that went along with visiting as they ate.

Barbara knew it was silly, but she felt out of place. Since she wasn't working in the harness shop, she had nothing to contribute to the conversation the men were having.

A sudden wave of dizziness hit Barbara with the force of a strong wind, and a need to sit swept over her. She had to eat something, even if her appetite was gone.

She moved slowly to the table and sat down.

"You get the little one settled?" her mother asked as she poured a glass of milk for Zachary.

Barbara reached for her water. "*Jah,* he's fast asleep again. Second nap this morning."

Mom studied Barbara intently. "I can see by the dark circles under your eyes that you're not gettin' enough sleep. Would it help if I started keepin' the older boys at our place during the night?"

Barbara took a bite of coleslaw, but it could have been shreds of straw for all the enjoyment she got from eating it. She knew why she was tired but didn't understand the feeling of depression she'd been plagued with or her lack of interest in food. It wasn't good for her or the baby.

"Daughter, did ya hear what I said about keepin' the boys overnight?"

"It's not the older ones keepin' me awake."

Mom reached across the table and patted Barbara's hand. "This *boppli* sleeps less than the others did, huh?"

Barbara nodded. "I wouldn't mind being up half the night if I could make up for it during the day. But I'm way behind paying the bills and sending out orders for supplies needed at the shop."

Paul spoke up. "Is there anything I can do to help? I'd be glad to send out the orders."

Barbara bristled as a dozen responses came to mind. *He's already doing my job in the shop, and now he wants to take over the paperwork, too?* She forced a polite smile while she shook her head. "Thanks for the offer, but I can manage."

Paul shrugged and grabbed another piece of ham.

Did he think she was unappreciative? Didn't the man realize how badly she needed to take part in her business?

She cut her meat and forked it into her mouth. *If*

43

only I wasn't so weak If I could work in the harness shop, I might not feel so depressed and useless. She felt like bursting into tears for no good reason. She swallowed the ham and washed it down with a gulp of water. *Am I experiencing postpartum depression, still missing David or just out of sorts because I'm feeling so drained?*

"Grandpa, can I help in the harness shop this afternoon?" Aaron asked.

"I reckon it would be all right if your *mamm* has no objections." Barbara's dad swung his gaze over to Paul. "And if it's okay with Paul."

A muscle along the side of Paul's cheek twitched, and he grunted.

Barbara was happy to hear her oldest boy had an interest in the shop again, but Paul seemed uncomfortable with the idea. "Aaron, maybe you should wait for another Saturday, when I'm back workin' in the shop," she suggested.

The boy's forehead wrinkled. "But that might take a long time. Grandma says you're real tired, and the *boppli*'s gonna need ya for a while. Ain't that so?"

Barbara couldn't deny it. She might not be able to return to work for several weeks yet. She pursed her lips in thought, uncertain how to respond. She didn't want Aaron worrying about her.

"Mama, can't I please work in the shop?" Aaron persisted.

Barbara glanced at Paul again to gauge his reaction. He looked as uncomfortable as when he'd first entered the room. "If Grandpa and Paul are both okay with it, then you can help a few hours this afternoon."

Paul reached up and rubbed his jaw. "Um—guess we could use some help cleaning up the place."

"Is that all?" Aaron scrunched up his nose. "I'll bet if my *daed* was still alive, he'd let me do some fun stuff. Always did before."

"We're out there to work, not have fun," Paul said with a frown.

Barbara stiffened. "You don't have to be so harsh with the boy. He meant no disrespect."

Paul's face turned bright red. "I was just stating facts."

"I think working in the harness shop is fun," she asserted.

Mom's head bobbed up and down. "That's right. Why, I can't tell ya how many times I've heard Barbara say how much fun she has in the shop. 'Course, that's not to say I agree with her. Personally, I think harness makin' is too hard for a woman, and I've told my daughter so many times."

It was obvious to Barbara that neither Paul nor her mother saw things the way she did. She grabbed a deviled egg and bit into it, determined to get her strength back. She was thankful for Paul's help, because Dad couldn't manage alone. But as soon as she was on her feet again, Barbara would be ready to take over the shop, and Paul Hilty could hightail it right back to Pennsylvania!

six

For the next few weeks, Barbara kept pretty much to herself. She was tempted to go out to the harness shop to see how things were going, but she didn't want to see Paul. She missed not joining her folks for their noon meal but was afraid he might be there. She didn't know why, but Paul Hilty made her feel uncomfortable and defensive.

Barbara stared out the kitchen window. Two Amish buggies were parked in front of the harness shop, as well as one pickup truck. Business was obviously picking up, and if Paul weren't helping out, they would probably have to turn customers away.

She drew in a deep breath. *Thank You, Lord, that I'm feelin' a little stronger and not so dizzy today.*

A knock at the front door drew her thoughts aside. "Now, who'd be usin' that door?" she muttered on her way out of the kitchen.

When Barbara opened the door, her friend Faith Hertzler greeted her.

"*Gude mariye,* Barbara. I brought ya one of Noah's lemon sponge pies," Faith said as she stepped into the living room.

"Good mornin' to you, too. The pie looks delicious."

Faith smiled, and her blue eyes twinkled. "Thought it might fatten ya up a bit. You're lookin' awful skinny these days."

Barbara took the pie and motioned Faith to take a

seat on the couch. "I'll put this in the refrigerator and bring us a cup of tea."

"Sounds *gut*. Oh, and there's a verse of scripture attached to the pie. I included a little joke on the back side of the paper, too."

Barbara nodded. "Figured as much."

A few minutes later, she returned with two cups of hot tea. She handed one to Faith and took a seat in the rocker across from her. "How come you used the front door and not the back?"

"Noah's out in the harness shop seein' about havin' some new bridles made. I saw your three boys playin' in the front yard and went there to visit a minute." Faith chuckled. "I was too lazy to walk around back after the children and I finished chattin'."

Barbara frowned. "Aaron's home from school already? Didn't realize it was that late."

"School let out early today. It's the last day of school, you know."

"Oh, that's right," Barbara said. "Where's your *kinner?* Are they out playin' with my three?"

Faith shook her head. "Left 'em with my folks so Noah and I could have a little time together. We're plannin' to go to Seymour and do some shoppin'; then he's taking me out for barbecued ribs."

"That sounds nice."

"It's been awhile since we did anything without our two young'uns along. Noah left Osborn's Tree Farm a little early since things are a bit slow there right now."

"I see."

Faith chuckled. "Melinda was real happy about going over to her grandma and grandpa Stutzman's, because her aunt Susie's cat just had a litter of kittens."

"Is Melinda still takin' in every stray animal that comes along?" Barbara asked.

"Oh, *jah.* That girl would turn our place into a zoo if we let her."

"She's never been one to sit around and play with dolls, has she?"

"Only the one her real *daed* gave her before he died. She hung on to that doll 'til I married Noah; then she finally put it away in a drawer."

"Must have lost interest in it."

Faith shrugged. "I tried to get her to play with the old faceless doll my *mamm* made when I was a girl, but she stuck that away, too."

Barbara took a sip of her tea. "Guess some girls would rather do other things than play mama."

Faith nodded. "Like me—the girl who grew up tellin' jokes and yodelin' and couldn't have cared less about domestic things."

"How's your boy doing these days?" Barbara asked. "Did he get over that awful cough he had?"

"Isaiah's fine now." Faith leaned forward and set her cup on the coffee table. "But I don't think you are."

Barbara felt her defenses rise. Had her friend come over to lecture her? "I'll get my weight back as soon as my appetite improves," she said through tight lips.

"You've got to eat enough for both you and little

David. Nursing mothers need plenty of nourishment, ya know."

"I'm fine. Still a little weak, but that's gettin' better. And I make myself eat even if I'm not hungry."

Faith clasped her hands around her knees. "How's your mental health?"

Barbara blinked as her friend's question hit her with the force of a tornado. "What are you gettin' at?"

"You're depressed. I can see it in your eyes and the way your shoulders slump."

Heat flooded Barbara's face. Faith knew her so well, but she hated to admit the way she felt. It was a sign of weakness to be depressed, and up until David died, she had always been strong. Even after he was killed, she'd managed to avoid the depression she now felt by keeping busy in the harness shop.

"It might help to talk about it," Faith prompted.

Barbara shuddered as tears clouded her vision. It wasn't like her to lose control. She usually did well at keeping everything boxed in. "Talkin' won't change a thing."

"Maybe not, but it might make ya feel better." Faith patted the sofa cushion. "Come sit by me and pour out your heart."

Barbara released a sigh and placed her cup on the small table to her left. She figured Faith wouldn't leave until she got what she came for, and she was pretty sure the woman's goal was to make her break down. Faith had said many times that God gave people tear ducts for a good reason, and folks shouldn't be too stubborn to use them.

When Barbara took a seat beside her friend, she clenched her fingers into a tight ball and willed herself not to cry.

"Is it postpartum depression?" Faith questioned. "Is that what you're dealin' with?"

"Maybe." Barbara felt her neck spasm as despair gripped her like a vise. "I think it's a combination of things."

"Such as?"

"Missin' David—feelin' bad because he will never know his youngest son—wantin' to be out at the harness shop but knowin' I'm too weak to do much more than care for myself and the baby."

"Your *mamm*'s lookin' after the other three, right?"

Barbara nodded.

"And Paul Hilty's helping in the shop, so that gives ya time to rest up and get your strength back."

"Jah."

"I don't mean to lecture, but you should be grateful for all the help."

Barbara crossed her arms to dispel the sudden chill she felt. A tear seeped out from under her lashes. "I am grateful, but I feel so guilty right now."

"Guilty for what?"

"I'm useless."

Faith reached over and squeezed Barbara's hand. "How can ya say that? The *boppli* needs ya to care for him and be strong."

"I know if I get plenty of rest and eat right, I'll regain strength physically. But I'm weak emotionally, too, and I don't know if I'll ever be strong again." A sob escaped Barbara's lips, and she clamped her mouth shut.

Faith gently patted Barbara's back. "Go ahead and get it out. Let the cleansin' tears come."

"Why do I feel guilty when I'm sad?" Barbara wailed.

"Maybe because you're used to being in control of things, and this is something you can't control."

Barbara couldn't deny the fact that she did like to be in charge. "But I wasn't like this before little Davey was born."

"Until now ya didn't have time to be depressed. Now that you're not working in the shop and you're being forced to slow down, your feelings are coming to the surface. Did you see the verse of scripture from Ecclesiastes that Noah attached to the pie? It reminds us there's a time for laughter and a time for tears."

Faith's last comment unleashed the dam. Barbara bent into her pain and wept for all she was worth. When her sobs finally tapered to sniffling hiccups, she reached for a tissue from the box on the coffee table and blew her nose. "Sorry for blubberin'."

"It's all right. God knows your pain, and you have every right to cry."

Barbara's gaze darted to the Bible lying on the coffee table. "My faith isn't strong anymore. Not the way yours seems to be."

Faith shook her head. "My faith wasn't always so strong. It used to be almost nonexistent. Remember how I was when I came home after livin' among the English, thinkin' I wanted to be famous and make lots of money as an entertainer?"

Barbara nodded. She did remember how life used to be for Faith. But her friend was a different person now, and God had blessed her in many ways. Noah was a wonderful, loving husband, and they had two beautiful, healthy children. Would Faith be as secure in her beliefs if she'd lost the man she loved? It was easy to talk about having faith in God when things were going well.

"I know it's wrong for me to feel this way, but I'm jealous of you, Faith," Barbara admitted.

"Why?"

"Your husband is alive, and everything's going great in your life."

Faith stared at the floor, her fingers kneading the folds in her dark green dress. "We've got our share of troubles, too."

Regret, as strong as a Missouri king snake, coiled around Barbara's middle. She'd been wallowing in self-pity, and here was her friend going through problems she didn't even know about. "What's wrong, Faith? Can you talk about it?"

Faith smiled, but her soulful blue eyes revealed the depth of her pain. "The doctor gave us the news at my last appointment. We can't have any more children."

Barbara's heart clenched. She knew how much her friend had hoped for another baby. "I'm awful sorry," she murmured.

"I've come to terms with it. At least I have Melinda and Isaiah, and I love 'em both very much."

"I know you do."

"If it were God's will for us to have more *kinner,* He would not have closed up my womb."

Barbara couldn't believe how matter-of-fact Faith was being. It reminded her of what Bishop Frey said on the day of David's funeral. *"Our faith teaches that when our time on earth is over, God will call us home no matter what. We just need to accept His will and move on with life."*

"You've come a long way from the rebellious teenager I used to know," Barbara said. "Your strong faith and positive attitude amaze me."

Faith gave Barbara a hug. "Your friendship is one of the things that helped me grow, and I want you to know that I'm here for you now."

Barbara dabbed at the corners of her eyes. *"Danki.* I appreciate that. But I'm sure once I return to work I'll be able to make it on my own again."

"It sure is *gut* to have you back in Webster County," Noah Hertzler said as he returned the strip of leather Paul said would work for the bridles he wanted.

Paul placed it on the workbench. "I'm not here for good, you know. Just working at the harness shop 'til Barbara's up to taking over again." He shook his head.

"Although it amazes me that any woman would want to do this kind of work."

Noah snickered. "I think some of the women in our community are cut from a different cloth than most."

"How so?"

"Take my wife, for instance. She loves to yodel and tell funny stories."

Paul nodded. "So I've heard."

"Not the everyday kind of thing you'd expect from an Amish woman, mind you. But that's what makes Faith so special." Noah grinned. "Then there's my stepdaughter, Melinda. That girl takes in every stray critter that comes near our place, and some I think she goes lookin' for."

Paul leaned against the workbench and laughed. "Sounds like you've got your hands full."

Noah smiled. "*Jah,* but in a *gut* way."

Paul could tell by the gleam in Noah's eyes that he was a happy man. He had a wife he obviously loved, a stepdaughter whose whims he catered to, a son to carry on his name, and a job at a tree farm, which Noah said he thoroughly enjoyed. All Paul had was a job in Lancaster County, working for his cousin, with little hope of ever owning his own business. He had no wife or children, and he wasn't getting any younger.

He'd turned thirty a few months ago, and most men his age were already married with three or four *kinner.*

"You enjoying the time spent with your folks while you're here?" Noah asked.

Paul shrugged. "Me and Pop haven't seen eye to eye

since I refused to take up farming. We can barely be in the same room without one of us snapping at the other."

"I know what you mean. My *daed* has never understood why I'd rather work at the tree farm than slop hogs with him." Noah folded his arms across his chest. "He's never understood my interest in baking, either. But I've come to realize some things probably won't change, and it's best to try and ignore them."

"Guess you're right," Paul said with a nod. "If I let Pop's grumbling get to me, I'd be on the next bus bound for Pennsylvania. But it wouldn't be right to run out on Barbara in her hour of need."

"I'm glad you're here for her." Noah glanced around. "Hey, where's Samuel?"

"He hired a driver to take him to Springfield for a doctor's appointment. I've been on my own all afternoon, and as you might have noticed when you first came in, the customers have kept me quite busy."

Noah nodded. "That's why I waited 'til the others left to start yakkin'."

Paul pointed to the stack of papers on the desk. "I work fast, but there's no way I can keep up with all the orders we have right now."

"If I knew anything about what you're doing here, I'd offer to help. But I'd probably just be in the way."

"That's okay. I'll be fine. Just need to 'keep my nose to the leather,' as my cousin Abe likes to say."

Noah snickered and turned toward the door. "Faith went up to the house to visit Barbara. Guess I'd better see if she's ready to head for Seymour. I'm taking my wife to eat supper at her favorite place—the Hillbilly Café."

"Have fun. I'll let you know when your bridles are ready."

"Danki."

When the door clicked shut behind Noah, Paul turned to the workbench, wishing it were him and Barbara going out to eat. He slapped the side of his face. "What's wrong with you, Paul Hilty? Get yourself busy and quit thinking such stupid thoughts!"

seven

Barbara stepped onto the back porch, preparing to air out a braided throw rug, in time to see John Frey's buggy pull into the yard. She thought he was headed to the harness shop until he pulled up to the hitching rail close to the house.

"Wie geht's?" the bishop called as he exited the buggy.

"I'm doin' all right. What brings you out our way?"

He joined her on the porch. "Just out for a drive and thought I'd check up on you." He smiled, tipping his straw hat. "How are things in the harness shop?"

"Paul Hilty's helpin' there right now. As far as I know, things are goin' okay."

"Will he be stayin' on?"

She gave the rug a good shake. "Just until I feel up to workin' again."

"That's *gut*." The bishop squinted against the sun shining in his gray-blue eyes; then he offered her another smile.

As Barbara draped the throw rug over the porch rail, an uncomfortable feeling settled over her. She didn't like the way Bishop Frey was looking at her. The man was a widower, nearly fifteen years her senior, with four teenage daughters to raise. When Jacob Martin passed on a year and a half ago, John took over as the new bishop for their district. Then six months ago, John's wife, Peggy, died of cancer. Barbara hoped John didn't plan on her being his new wife. She had no plans to marry again. Besides, she couldn't imagine having to deal with teenagers right now. She had her hands full taking care of four boys.

"You're lookin' a mite peaked," the bishop said. "If you're needin' some help with the baby, I could send one of the girls over. Betty and Nadine both have jobs, but I'm sure either Mary or Hannah could come."

Barbara shook her head. "I appreciate the offer, but Mom's helping with the three older boys, and I'm managing okay with the *boppli*."

John glanced around the yard with scrutinizing eyes. "Looks like you could use some help outside."

Barbara couldn't argue with that. Since David died, the lawn and flower beds had been dreadfully neglected. Her father wasn't able to keep up with yard work and help in the harness shop, too. Mom had a weak back, so she had trouble bending over to pull weeds. The lawn only got cut when Dad felt up to it and had the time. The flower beds would have to stay full of weeds until a group of ladies from the community showed up for a workday, as they'd promised.

"We're gettin' by," Barbara mumbled, feeling a knot form in her stomach.

"Are you sure? I'd be right happy to have one of my daughters come over."

Barbara gritted her teeth and concentrated on the patterns of light that dappled the porch floor. "I'll let you know."

John leaned against the railing opposite the rug, apparently in no hurry to leave. "I was wonderin' if you and the boys would care to go on a picnic Saturday afternoon."

The knot in her stomach tightened. "I appreciate the offer, but I don't think the *boppli*'s ready for that kind of an outing."

"Couldn't you leave him with your *mamm* for a few hours?"

Barbara's face grew warm. She could hardly remind the bishop that she had to stay close to Davey because she was nursing.

As if by divine intervention, she heard the little guy start to fuss. "I've got to go inside now. The *boppli*'s cryin'." She turned toward the door. "It was kind of you to drop by."

"What about the picnic?"

When Barbara glanced over her shoulder, the scrutiny she saw on the bishop's face made her feel even more uncomfortable than when he'd examined her overrun yard. She forced her lips into what she hoped was a polite smile. "I appreciate the offer, but it's really not possible. Good day, Bishop John." Barbara hurried into the house before he could say anything more.

A few minutes later, she lifted the baby from the portable crib she kept in the living room. "The bishop probably thought I was rude, but I couldn't let you keep on cryin'," she murmured against the infant's downy head. "Besides, I'm not about to give that man any hope of me becomin' his wife."

Paul hated to bother Barbara, but he had several orders that needed to be sent, and she'd made it clear when she hired him that she would be placing all the orders. He'd thought about asking Samuel to take the paperwork up to the house, but the older man had left early that morning for another doctor's appointment in Springfield.

Since there were no customers at the moment, Paul decided this was a good time to take the information up to Barbara. He put the Closed sign in the shop window with a note saying they'd be open again after lunch.

Paul stepped onto the back porch of Barbara's house, prepared to knock on the door, hand her the papers, and get right back to the harness shop, where he would eat his lunch in peace and quiet.

As he lifted his hand to knock, he heard a child's voice ask, "Whatcha doin'?"

Paul whirled around. Barbara's six-year-old, Joseph, stood beside a bush near the porch, holding a bubble wand in his hand.

"I . . . uh . . . need to see your *mamm*," Paul stammered. He didn't know why he always felt tongue-tied when he was around children.

"She's in the house."

Paul nodded. "I figured she might be."

"You come over for lunch?" Joseph asked, his dark eyes looking ever so serious.

"No. I'm here on business."

Joseph stepped onto the porch. "Mama's harness business?"

"*Jah.*"

The boy turned the doorknob and called through the open doorway, "Mama, the harness man's here to see you!"

Paul felt as though he'd be intruding if he stepped into the house without an invitation, so he waited on the porch.

When Barbara showed up, several strands of dark hair had worked their way loose from the *kapp* on her head. "Is there a problem at the shop?"

"No. I just wanted to give you these." Paul handed her the folder full of supply orders.

"*Danki.* I'll get everything sent out right away."

Joseph tossed the bubble wand onto a small table on the porch and yanked on the hem of his mother's apron. "Can the harness man stay for lunch? We've got plenty, right?"

Barbara's face flamed. "His name is Paul, and I'm sure he's busy."

Joseph shook his head. "No, he ain't. There's no cars or buggies parked in front of the shop." He pointed out back.

A trickle of sweat rolled down Paul's forehead, and he reached up to wipe it away.

"If you haven't already eaten, you're welcome to join us," Barbara said, much to Paul's surprise.

Whatever she was cooking in the kitchen smelled mighty good. He licked his lips. "Well, I—"

"Mama's fixin' chicken noodle soup," Joseph said. "It's awful *gut.*"

Paul couldn't help but smile at the boy's enthusiasm. "If you're sure it's no trouble," he said to Barbara. "Maybe we could talk about business while we eat."

Barbara nodded. "Sounds fine to me."

Paul stepped inside, and she shut the door.

"Was that Bishop Frey I saw here earlier?" Paul asked as he followed her into the kitchen.

Barbara nodded. "He came by to see how I was doin'."

"Guess that's part of his duties."

"*Jah.*" Barbara motioned to the table. "Why don't you have a seat? If the *boppli* doesn't wake from his nap right away, I'll have the soup ready in no time."

"Is there something I can do to help?" Paul offered. Anything would be better than sitting at the table watching the woman bustle around the kitchen. Every time Paul saw Barbara Zook, he thought she was prettier than the time before. Gone were the dark circles under her eyes, and if he wasn't mistaken, she'd put on a few needed pounds.

"Guess you could go out back and call my other two boys in for lunch. Aaron's pushin' Zachary on the swing behind the barn."

"I can get 'em, Mama," Joseph said.

"If I send you, Aaron will only argue, or you'll end up gettin' sidetracked along the way."

"The boys aren't over at your folks' place today?" Paul asked.

"Mom went to Springfield with Dad."

"Of course."

"I think she asks that doctor more questions than my *daed* ever does. He tends to go along with whatever the doctor says and never thinks to voice any concerns."

"I think most men are like that." Paul opened the back door. "I'll go get your boys."

He'd only gone as far as the barn when he noticed Joseph beside him. "I thought you were inside with your *mamm.*"

"Wanted to be with you."

Paul wasn't sure how to respond, so he kept walking. He'd never been good with children, and until recently, none had ever shown an interest in him. Truth be told, it felt kind of nice.

He heard squeals of laughter and looked up to see Aaron pushing his little brother on the swing.

"Your *mamm* wants you to come up to the house," he said. "She's got lunch about ready."

Aaron stopped pushing the younger boy and whirled around to face Paul. "How come she sent you?"

"The harness man's stayin' for lunch," Joseph announced.

Paul felt Aaron's icy stare all the way to his toes. It was clear the boy did not like him, though he didn't know why. After Paul began working at the harness shop, Aaron had dropped by a couple of times after school and on Saturdays, wanting to help out. Paul had noticed that Aaron only came around when his grandfather was there. When Paul was minding the shop alone, the boy stayed away. It was just as well. Aaron only would have been in the way, and Paul had too much work to spend time baby-sitting.

Guess that's sort of what I'm doin' right now, he thought as he looked at Joseph, who stared up at him with eager brown eyes. *Maybe I need to reach out to Aaron.*

"Come on, Zachary," Aaron said as he helped his little brother off the swing. "It's time to eat." He grabbed the boy's hand, and the two of them scampered toward the house.

Joseph reached for Paul's hand, and they followed the other boys. Paul found it interesting that one of Barbara's sons could be so friendly while the other seemed so aloof. Was Aaron missing his father? Could that be the problem?

"Say, Aaron," Paul said as he and Joseph stepped onto the porch. "How would you like to come out to the harness shop after lunch and help me?"

"Doin' what?" he asked without looking back. "Sweepin' the floor again?"

When Paul touched the boy's shoulder, he halted and turned around. "Thought you might like to fasten buckles on some leather straps, or maybe dye the edges."

A flicker of interest sparked in Aaron's eyes, but when he blinked it disappeared. "We'll see," he mumbled.

As they entered the kitchen, Paul noticed that Barbara had set the table and lunch was ready. The welcome aroma of chicken noodle soup teased Paul's nose and made his stomach growl. A hot, home-cooked meal would be a heap better than the sandwich lying in his lunch box back at the shop.

Barbara motioned to the chair at the head of the table. "Have a seat, Paul."

"But that's Papa's place," Aaron was quick to say. "Nobody should sit there 'cept Papa."

"Aaron, your *daed*'s gone, and—"

Paul shook his head. "It's all right, Barbara. I can sit someplace else." He waited until Aaron and Joseph took their seats and Barbara put Zachary on a high stool. After she was seated, Paul took the empty chair across from her.

All heads bowed. When the silent prayer was over, Barbara passed Paul a basket of rolls.

"These look good. Did you make them?" he asked.

"My friend Faith Hertzler brought them over yesterday. Her husband likes to bake, so she often brings me special treats."

Paul took a roll and slathered it with butter. "*Jah,* I've heard about Noah's tasty baked goods."

"I haven't had the energy to do much baking since the *boppli* was born," Barbara commented.

"You'll get your strength back soon. Already you're looking better than the day I first dropped by."

She smiled. "I'm anxious to get back to the harness shop. I surely do miss it."

Paul was tempted to ask why she felt the need to do men's work, but he thought better of it. He would be going back to Pennsylvania soon, and what she did was her own business. Besides, she needed a way to support herself, and according to her *daed,* Barbara was good at her trade.

He dipped his spoon into the soup and took a mouthful. "Mmm . . . this is mighty good."

"*Danki.*"

Joseph smacked his lips. "Mama's the best cook in all of Webster County."

Barbara snickered. "*Jah,* sure."

Paul glanced at Aaron, who sat to his mother's left. The boy had his head down and seemed to be playing with his soup, stirring it over and over with his spoon.

"Aaron, you'd best eat and quit dawdlin'," Barbara scolded.

The child picked up his bowl and slurped his soup, the way Paul did whenever he used a mug.

"Mind your manners and use your spoon." Barbara handed a roll to young Zachary, and he promptly dipped it in his soup.

"Would it be all right if Aaron comes out to the shop after lunch?" Paul asked. "With your *daed* being gone today, I could use some help."

Barbara's look of concern made him wish he hadn't said anything. "Are you gettin' further behind?"

He shook his head. "Just thought an extra pair of hands would be nice."

Barbara turned to face Aaron. "Would you mind helpin' Paul this afternoon?"

His only response was a slight shrug.

"All right, then. But you must do everything Paul says, is that clear?"

"Jah."

Paul gripped his spoon. *I may regret asking the boy to help as much as I wish I hadn't accepted Barbara's invitation to lunch.* He knew it was silly, but being this close to her made him long for something he could never have. He decided to forgo talking about the harness business over lunch. *As soon as I finish this bowl of soup, I'm gonna hightail it right back to work.*

eight

Barbara curled up on her bed, glad that the baby, Zachary, and Joseph were taking naps. Since Aaron was out at the harness shop with Paul, that meant she also had time to rest. She had done too much earlier in the day and felt exhausted by the time they'd finished eating lunch. Paul had offered to help her with the dishes, but she knew he needed to get back to the shop, so she declined, saying she could manage on her own. She'd ended up leaving the dishes soaking in the sink, deciding she could do them later, when she hopefully would have a little more energy.

As Barbara burrowed into the pillow, a vision of Paul popped into her head. She had been avoiding him lately because he made her feel uncomfortable. Today at lunch, however, she'd actually enjoyed his company.

Joseph seemed taken with him, she mused. Fact was, the boy hung on Paul's every word.

"It's not fair, Mama," Joseph had wailed when Barbara said he needed a nap. *"If Aaron gets to help in the harness shop, I should, too."*

Barbara grinned. Joseph was nearly six, but not old enough to help in the shop. Then again, she didn't think Aaron was thrilled about helping Paul. It would be good for the boy, though. Good for him to spend time alone with another man besides his grandpa.

Aaron misses his daed. *But he can learn from Paul the way he did David* She rolled onto her side. *If I'm feeling up to it after my nap, maybe I'll bundle up the baby and take a walk out there and see how things are goin'.* She was sure everything was all right, but it would be good to see for herself.

Barbara thought about her husband. David had enjoyed running the harness shop. He'd said many times that their firstborn would take over the business someday. Even when Aaron was a toddler, David had invited the boy out there just to let him hold the leather straps and "get the feel of things."

Tears welled up in Barbara's eyes. How she missed working in the shop with her beloved husband. She missed their long talks after the children were put to bed, and she pined for the physical touch of the man she had loved since she was a teenager. Would she ever know love like that again?

"I could never feel for the bishop what I felt for David," she whispered against the wedding-ring quilt on her bed. It had been a gift from her *mamm* when she and David got married. "Don't know that I could ever feel such love for any man but my David."

Heavy with the need for sleep, Barbara's eyelids closed. As she started to drift off, David's image was replaced with that of Paul Hilty. The way he'd smiled at her during lunch made her heart feel lighter than it had in many weeks. A chunk of blond hair kept falling onto his forehead, and she had to resist the temptation to push it back in place, the way she often did with one of her boys. The last thing Barbara saw as she succumbed to sleep was the vision of Aaron and Paul walking side by side toward the harness shop.

Paul peered over Aaron's shoulder as the boy reached for a buckle from the box sitting in the middle of the workbench. "Not that one, Aaron. It's too big for the size strap you're working on."

The boy grunted and grabbed another buckle. As he fumbled with the clasp and tried to fasten it to the leather strap, it slipped and fell on the floor.

"Be careful now." Paul stooped to retrieve the buckle.

"It was slippery," Aaron complained.

"Maybe you've got linseed oil on your hands from when you were oiling that saddle earlier."

"Nope. I washed 'em."

"Could be you didn't wash well enough. Might be a good idea to do it again, son."

Aaron spun around, his dark eyes smoldering. "You ain't my *daed*."

The tips of Paul's ears warmed, the way they always did when he was flustered. "'Course not. Never said I was."

"But ya called me 'son.'"

Paul shrugged. "Just a figure of speech."

"And you've been tellin' me what to do ever since we came out to my *daed*'s shop."

"If you're going to be my helper, then I have the right to tell you what to do."

Aaron frowned and squinted his eyes, then turned and headed for the sink at the back of the shop. Paul shook his head. *Maybe asking the boy to help out wasn't such a good idea. Might be best if I sent him back to the house.* Paul opened his mouth to say so, but the front door swung open and Noah Hertzler stepped into the shop.

"I got off work early today and was passing by on my way home," Noah said, "so thought I'd stop and see how you're comin' with those bridles I ordered."

"Should be ready by next week," Paul answered.

Noah nodded toward the back of the building. "I see you've got yourself a helper."

Paul grimaced. "I believe he likes being in the shop, but I don't think he cottons to me so well."

"Give him time. He'll come around."

"Did he help his *daed* much?"

Noah nodded. "He followed David around like he was his shadow, though I'm not sure how much help he was in the shop. Never seen a father and son so close as those two seemed to be."

"Wish I could say the same for me and my *daed*."

"Still havin' problems?"

"Yep. Just last night we got into a disagreement over me returning to Pennsylvania."

Noah's eyebrows furrowed. "You leavin' soon?"

Paul shook his head. "Not 'til Barbara's back working again."

"You think it'll be much longer?"

"Don't rightly know. She invited me to eat lunch with her and the boys today, and she seemed to be doing okay." He frowned. "Come to think of it, she did look kind of tired by the time we were done."

"She's been through a lot."

Paul nodded.

"Guess your brother's widow must still be grieving, too."

"*Jah.*"

"Been several deaths in our community lately." Noah stuffed his hands into his pants pockets. "John Frey lost his wife six months ago."

"I heard that."

Noah's voice lowered a notch. "Word has it he's lookin' for another wife already."

Paul leaned against the workbench and crossed his arms. "Is that so?"

"Yep. He's got four teenage daughters who need a woman's guiding hand."

"I suppose they would."

"Faith thinks the bishop has set his cap for Barbara."

Paul's mouth dropped open. That would explain John Frey's visit earlier in the day. Apparently the man had more on his mind than just checking to see how she was doing.

"You look surprised," Noah said. "It's pretty common for a widower with *kinner* to remarry soon after his wife's passing. Truth be told, I'm surprised Barbara hasn't married by now, what with her havin' three young'uns and a *boppli* to raise. Not to mention her needin' help here in the shop."

Paul gave a slight shrug. The thought of Barbara marrying Bishop Frey made his stomach churn. She was too young and full of life to be married to a man whose hair and beard had more gray in it than brown. As he opened his mouth to say something, Aaron came sauntering up, holding his hands out for inspection. "See, no oil."

"That's *gut*. Why don't you get back to work on them buckles, then?"

Aaron glanced up at Noah. "Did ya bring any cookies today?"

Noah shook his head. "Not this time." He motioned toward the workbench. "Want to show me what you've been workin' on?"

"Ain't nothin' much, but if ya wanna see, it's all right by me."

When Noah winked, Paul grinned and stepped aside. Aaron led Noah over to the bench while Paul went to work at the riveting machine, where he would press metal rivets into a leather strap. He was thankful Noah had dropped by. Aaron seemed much more comfortable with him. *Maybe I need to try harder with the boy.*

When Barbara awoke from her nap, she discovered Joseph and Zachary playing in their room. Aaron was nowhere to be found, so she assumed he was still at the shop with Paul. The baby was awake but not fussy. She would change his diaper and see if he wanted to nurse; then the four of them would go check on Aaron.

Half an hour later, Barbara headed to the harness shop. She held the baby in her arms while Zachary and Joseph traipsed alongside her.

When they entered the harness shop, the sight that greeted Barbara sent a shock through her middle. Aaron's hands were black, and he had dark smudges on his face and shirt. He held on to a strap, which he'd obviously been staining, but the child had more dye on himself than anyplace else. She looked around for Paul. He stood in front of the riveting machine, humming and working away like he didn't have a care in the world. Didn't the man realize what a mess Aaron had made? He'd obviously not been watching the boy very closely. Maybe Barbara had made a mistake agreeing to let Aaron help Paul.

"What's wrong, Mama?" Aaron asked. "Ya look kinda *grank*."

Barbara moved swiftly to his side, and the younger boys followed. "I'm not sick, Aaron, just a bit put out."

"How come?"

"Look at your hands."

"Yeah, they're black as coal," Joseph put in.

"Black as coal," Zachary parroted.

Aaron wrinkled his nose. "Stay out of this, Joseph."

"I'm only statin' facts," Joseph said with a sneer.

Barbara shifted the baby to her other arm and nodded at Aaron. "I want you to march on back to the sink and scrub your hands and face."

"But, Mama, I ain't done yet, and Paul said if I finished this job by four o'clock, he'd pay me a dollar."

Barbara had to admit Aaron seemed to be enjoying himself. She didn't want to say anything that might cause him to dislike working in the harness shop. After all, the business would be his someday if he wanted it. "All right, then. But try to be more careful. It's the leather ends you're supposed to be staining, not your hands and clothes."

He grinned up at her. "I'll do my best."

She moved toward Paul, but the two younger boys

stayed near Aaron. That was just as well. She didn't think they should hear what she had to say.

"Come to see how Aaron's doing?" Paul asked when she stood in front of the riveting machine.

Barbara nodded. "He's making a real mess with that dye you're letting him use."

"Dying leather's a messy job."

"*Jah,* but his hands are all black, and he ended up gettin' dye on his shirt and face, too."

Paul didn't say anything, just kept working.

"Did you show him the right way to hold the brush and cover the edges of the leather with stain?"

"Of course."

When the baby hiccupped, Barbara put him over her shoulder and patted his back. "There's a right way and a wrong way to hold the paintbrush," she said. "The right way keeps the stain on the leather and not so much on the hands."

Paul's pale eyebrows drew together. "Are you questioning my ability to teach your son?"

She clamped her lips shut, afraid she might spew some unkind words. Who did Paul Hilty think he was? He acted as if this were his shop.

"Well, are you?" he persisted.

Barbara drew in a deep breath and blew it out quickly. "I'm not questionin' your ability. But I think you need to remember that this is *my* shop, and Aaron is *my* son." She paused long enough to grab another quick breath. "Not only that, but I'm the one who will have to spend time trying to get the dye off his hands and face before Sunday comes. Sure wouldn't want him going to preaching like that."

Paul chuckled. "No, that would never do."

Barbara bit her bottom lip so hard she noticed the metallic taste of blood. "Are you laughin' at me?"

"Not really." His smile widened. "I was just thinking how cute you look when you're mad."

Her face heated up. "I am not mad." *And he shouldn't be saying I'm cute. I'm a married woman, for goodness' sake. Well, I used to be.*

"You're not mad, huh? Then how come your cheeks are so pink?"

Barbara mentally counted to ten. Was he trying to goad her into an argument? "I'm upset because you haven't been watchin' Aaron close enough."

"I have been watching him, and the boy's doing fine, Barbara. I know he made a mess with the dye, but how is he supposed to learn if he doesn't try?"

In her heart Barbara knew Paul was right. Aaron would learn best by doing, even if he did make a mess. Despite her rationalization, she still felt defensive. This was her shop, and she had a certain way of doing things. That included how she would teach her son to dye leather straps.

"I'm thinkin' sometime next week I might come to the shop and work awhile," she blurted out.

Paul's eyebrows lifted. "You really think that's wise? It's only been a few weeks since you had the baby."

Her heart began to pound. Did he think he knew

what was best for her, too? "I'm not plannin' to work full time. Just thought it would be good to try a few hours and see how it goes."

"What about the *kinner?*"

"My mom will watch them."

"Even the *boppli?* Doesn't he need to be fed regularly?"

She nodded. "I can plan my time in the shop around his feeding schedule. If he needs me, Mom can always send one of the boys out to the shop to let me know."

Paul shrugged and grabbed another metal rivet. "Whatever you think best. You're the boss."

nine

Sunday dawned with a cloudless sky, and for the first time since little David was born, Barbara would be going to church. In some ways she looked forward to it, as she'd missed fellowshipping with other believers. But in a way, she looked on it with dread. Paul would no doubt be there, and after their confrontation at the harness shop the other day, she wasn't sure she could face him.

She stood by the kitchen window, staring at the overgrown lawn. *He probably thinks I'm rude and controlling, but he has to understand the way things are. I own the harness shop, and that gives me the right to say how things should be done. I'm also Aaron's mother, and regardless of what Paul may think, I do know what's best for my son.*

A vision of her oldest boy's dirty black hands popped into Barbara's mind. When Aaron had come home from the shop that day, she'd scrubbed for nearly an hour, trying to get the black stain off. The child's face came clean enough, and his hands did look some better. But three days later, there was still the telltale sign that he'd been working with dark stain. Instead of coal black, Aaron's hands were now a dingy gray.

Barbara looked away from the window when her three boys came running into the kitchen.

"Is breakfast ready yet, Mama?" Joseph asked. "I'm hungry!"

She smiled and pointed to the table. "I made blueberry pancakes."

"Yum. My favorite," Aaron said as he pulled out a chair.

"Did you wash?" Barbara asked.

He shook his head. "Didn't think I needed to this mornin'."

"Oh? And why's that?"

Aaron held up his hands. "Been washed so many times, there ain't much skin left."

"Don't exaggerate, son." Barbara nodded toward the sink.

Aaron grunted but did as he was told.

"Me and Zachary washed our hands," Joseph said.

"That's good. Now scoot up to the table." Barbara lifted Zachary onto his stool while Joseph sat in a chair. At least two of her boys were compliant. *Wonder how little David will be when he's older?* she mused. *Will he be even-tempered like these two, or will the* boppli *take after his oldest brother and be stubborn as a mule?*

"It's good to see ya this mornin'," Faith said as she helped Barbara climb down from her folks' buggy with the baby in her arms. The boys had already run off toward a group of children taking turns on the swing in Faith's side yard.

Barbara smiled. "It feels good to be out again. When I heard the service was being held at your place today, I couldn't resist coming."

"Why's that?"

"Figured there'd be lots of good food."

Faith snickered. "*Jah,* my Noah has seen to that, all right." She held out her hands. "Mind if I hold the baby? It's been awhile since I had a newborn in my arms."

Barbara handed her son over to Faith. "I believe he's put on a few pounds since you last saw him."

"That's *gut.*" Faith scrutinized Barbara. "Looks like you've gained some weight, too."

Barbara nodded. "I believe I have. My appetite's slowly returning."

"Glad to hear it. How's the depression?"

"It comes and goes. But I'm sure it'll be gone once I'm able to work in the harness shop again."

"How long do you think that will be?" Faith asked as they started toward the house.

"I'm hopin' to work a few hours next week."

Faith's eyebrows rose. "So soon?"

Barbara shrugged. "I get bored sittin' around the house all the time."

"But you have this little guy to keep you busy. Not to mention those three active boys." Faith motioned to the maple tree where the children awaited their turn on the swing.

"I know, and I love caring for my *kinner*. But I also like workin' in the shop." Barbara drew in a quick breath. "Besides, somebody's got to earn the money to support my brood."

"According to Noah, Paul's managing the harness shop just fine," Faith said when they stepped onto the front porch.

"He probably is, but he won't be here forever. I'm sure he's anxious to return to Pennsylvania. And until I'm workin' full time, I doubt he'll feel free to go."

"Shows what kind of man he is, don't ya think?" Faith took a seat in the rocking chair and began to rock the baby.

Barbara sat in the wicker chair next to her. "He seems conscientious and hardworkin'."

"Is that all?"

"What are you gettin' at?"

Faith tipped her head. "I merely wondered what you think of him as a man, that's all."

"I just told you."

"Does he appeal to ya?"

Barbara's mouth dropped open. She had no idea her friend was entertaining such thoughts about her and Paul. "It's not proper for a newly widowed woman to even think of such things, and you know it."

"Barbara, it's been almost a year since David died. Many widows and widowers marry within the first year."

Barbara stiffened. "I'm not lookin' for a husband."

"Maybe not. But I'm pretty sure there's one looking for you." Faith nodded toward Bishop Frey, who was heading their way. "I hear tell he's got marryin' on his mind, and word has it, you're his first choice."

Before Barbara could respond, the bishop stepped onto the porch. "*Gude mariye,* ladies," he said with a nod and a smile in Barbara's direction.

"Mornin', Bishop Frey," the women said in unison.

His eyebrows furrowed, and he gave his graying beard a little tug. "You're lookin' tired today, Barbara. Sure you don't want me to send one of the girls over to your place to help out?"

She forced a smile. "I'm managing, thank you. I'll let you know if I should need anything."

"I'll be around to call on you again."

"Danki."

"I'd best be gettin' inside now. Service will be starting soon." The bishop opened the front door and stepped inside.

Faith shifted the baby to her other arm. "What'd I tell you, Barbara? He's got his mind set on you, and that's for certain sure."

Barbara shrugged and reached for little David. "We'd better round up our *kinner* and get them seated."

"You're right. If I know Melinda, she's probably off

80

someplace with one of her pets, and Isaiah's most likely playin' with your boys." Faith left the rocking chair and headed into the yard, with Barbara following close behind.

From where he sat on the men's side of the room, Paul had the perfect view of Barbara Zook. She looked serene, sitting there on the bench, cradling her son in her arms. A deep yearning, almost an ache, welled up in his chest, just as it had that afternoon in her kitchen. Had he made a mistake thinking marriage wasn't for him? Should he look for a wife when he returned to Pennsylvania? He wasn't getting any younger. If he were going to marry and start a family, it should be soon. But was there anyone back home he was interested in? No other woman had ever affected him the way Barbara had. But his attraction to her made no sense. They'd never gone anywhere together socially. And whenever they were in the same room, he felt either uncomfortable or irritated with her criticism.

Paul forced his gaze away from Barbara and tried to focus on Bishop Frey's sermon. Hearing God's Word was why he'd come to church after all.

" 'Lo, children are an heritage of the Lord: and the fruit of the womb is his reward. As arrows are in the hand of a mighty man; so are children of the youth. Happy is the man that hath his quiver full of them: they shall not be ashamed, but they shall speak with the enemies in the gate.' Psalm 127:3-5," the bishop read from the Bible he held in his hands. "And chapter

128, verse 1, says, 'Blessed is every one that feareth the Lord; that walketh in his ways.' " He smiled. "Be fruitful and multiply and be blessed."

Paul shifted uncomfortably. Were the bishop's words directed at him? Was God speaking through John Frey, telling Paul he should get married and raise a family, and that by so doing, he would be blessed?

He thought about his conversation with Noah Hertzler the other day. Noah had mentioned the bishop's interest in Barbara. Maybe the man's sermon was directed at himself. Could be that John thought if he took another wife and had more children, he'd be twice blessed. That wife could turn out to be Barbara Zook.

I've got to quit thinking about this, Paul reprimanded himself. *If the bishop should marry Barbara, it's none of my business. She has the right to choose whoever she pleases.* He shuddered. *Then why does the idea of her becoming the bishop's wife make me feel so miserable?*

When the noon meal was over, Barbara put the baby and Zachary down for a nap. She was glad Faith had a crib available; she wouldn't feel comfortable leaving the infant on a bed or the couch with pillows propped around him. There was too much chance he could smother.

Barbara stared at her youngest son, sleeping peacefully on his side, and a lump formed in her throat. She knew she was more protective of him than she had been with her other three. Maybe it was because this little guy had no father and would never know the wonderful man for whom he'd been named. Or maybe it was her own insecurities. Ever since David had been snatched away so suddenly, she'd been a little paranoid. What if something bad happened to one of the *kinner?* What if she died and left them with no mother? Sure, her folks would step in and raise the boys, but they were getting up in years. Her four married sisters might be willing to take the boys, but two of them lived near Sweet Springs, and the other two had moved to Minnesota. It would be hard on the *kinner* to move from the only home they'd ever known.

Try not to worry, she admonished herself. *As Bishop Frey often quotes from the book of Matthew: " 'Which of you by taking thought can add one cubit unto his stature?' "*

Barbara turned away from the crib and tiptoed out of the room. She needed to give the future of her sons over to God and get on with her life. She decided to go outside in the fresh air and enjoy the rest of the day.

As soon as Barbara stepped onto the front porch, she spotted Paul. He was sitting on the grass under a maple tree, with Joseph in his lap. Her heart nearly melted at the sight. He looked so natural holding her son, and Joseph appeared as contented as a cat lying in a patch of sun.

I need to speak with Paul, she told herself. *Need to apologize for my abruptness the other day.*

Barbara stepped off the porch and walked swiftly across the lawn before she lost her nerve.

"Hi, Mama," Joseph said with a wide smile. "Me and the harness man—I mean, Paul—are plannin' a fishin' trip." Paul's ears turned pink, and he gave Barbara a sheepish grin. "Guilty as charged. I thought maybe next Saturday, after I close the shop in the afternoon."

Before she could respond, Joseph thumped the spot beside him. "Have a seat, and we'll tell ya about it."

Barbara knelt next to her son.

"I heard there's some pretty nice catfish in the pond over by Ben Swartley's place," Paul said. "Thought it might be fun to take the boys fishing." He motioned to Barbara. "You're welcome to come along if you like."

The thought of going fishing was like honey in Barbara's mouth. She hadn't been on such an outing in over a year. Not since David had taken her and the boys to the pond for a picnic a few weeks before his death.

"It sounds like fun," she said. "But I couldn't leave Davey that long."

"You wouldn't have to," Paul said. "You could bring the baby along."

"Yeah, Mama, the *boppli* can come, too," Joseph agreed.

Barbara shook her head. "I can't allow him to be in the sun all day."

"We could put up a tent," Paul suggested. "We'll set his baby carriage inside, and he'll be just fine."

Barbara had some netting she could drape over the

carriage to keep the bugs away, so maybe it would work after all. It would be nice to get away for a little while and do something fun. But did she really want to spend several hours alone with Paul? *Of course,* she reasoned, *I wouldn't really be alone with him. The boys will be there, too.*

"Can we go, Mama? Please?"

Joseph's question pulled Barbara's thoughts aside. She patted his shoulder. "I'll think on it. In the meantime, I'd like you to go find Aaron."

"What for? He don't wanna play with me; he said so."

"Tell him I want to head home soon."

Joseph's lower lip protruded. "Aw, do we have to?"

"Jah."

The boy stood, turned, and squeezed Paul around the neck. It was obvious he'd taken a liking to the man, and from the way Paul responded by patting Joseph on the back, Barbara was fairly sure the feeling was mutual.

As Joseph skipped away, Barbara searched for the necessary words to say to Paul. "I . . . uh . . . owe you an apology for the other day."

His eyebrows rose.

"I shouldn't have been so testy about Aaron's black hands, and I didn't mean to question your judgment. I hope you'll accept my apology."

A slow smile spread across Paul's face, and a familiar longing crept into her heart. *David used to look at me like that.*

"No apology needed," Paul said. "Aaron's your son, and you had a right to be concerned."

"*Danki.* I appreciate your understanding."

He plucked a blade of grass and stuck it between his teeth. "Sure hope you'll give some consideration to the fishing trip."

Barbara was taken aback by the stark emotion she saw in Paul's eyes.

"I will give it some thought," she murmured.

ten

On Monday morning Barbara had been too tired to think of walking to the harness shop, much less do any work there. It wasn't until Wednesday that she felt up to the task, and even then, she knew it could only be for an hour or two. She would wait until lunch was over, then take the three younger ones to her folks' place so Mom could watch them. She figured Aaron might like to help in the shop, too.

Knowing the three older boys were out front blowing bubbles, Barbara opened the door and stepped outside to call them in for lunch.

"There's a buggy comin', Mama," Aaron said.

She turned and saw Bishop Frey, and he wasn't heading to the harness shop. Instinctively, she reached up to straighten her head covering.

"*Wie geht's?*" the bishop called as he stepped down from the buggy.

"I'm fine, and you?" she replied.

"Hot and thirsty." He swiped his hand across his forehead. "It's a real scorcher today."

Barbara nodded toward the porch swing. "If you'd like to have a seat, I'll get you a glass of iced tea."

He grinned and seated himself on the swing. "I'd be much obliged."

Barbara wasn't sure whether to leave her boys with Bishop John or take them inside with her. Seeing how much fun Zachary was having as he raced back and forth, popping his brother's bubbles, she decided to leave things as they were. "I'll be right back," she said before hurrying inside.

A few minutes later she returned with a glass of iced tea for the bishop and some crackers for the boys. That should tide them over until lunch, and maybe keep their mouths too busy to talk. Barbara knew how chatty Joseph could be, and the last thing she needed was for him to tell John Frey any of their personal business.

She gave the boys their crackers and instructed them to go play in the barn awhile. As soon as they were gone, she handed the bishop his glass of iced tea.

"*Danki.*" He nodded at her. "Won't you sit with me and visit awhile?"

Barbara's skin prickled as she sensed this was more than a casual visit. She sat down in the wicker chair on the other side of the porch.

"I don't bite, ya know," he said with a crooked grin.

She forced a smile in return. "I'm sure you don't. But I want to be close to the back door so I can hear the *boppli* if he starts to cry."

He shrugged and removed his straw hat, using it to fan his face. "Whew! Sure hope it cools down some. It's only the beginnin' of June, and already it's hotter than an oven."

She nodded. "*Jah,* hot and sticky."

The bishop cleared his throat a couple of times and balanced his hat on his knees. "I've been thinkin' about the two of us."

The speed of Barbara's heartbeat picked up as she waited for him to continue.

"You've been widowed almost a year now, and it's been six months since my wife died." He paused a moment and licked his lips. "The book of Ecclesiastes says, 'Two are better than one; because they have good reward for their labour.' "

Her only response was a polite nod. She wasn't about to admit to the bishop that she'd read that same verse not long ago. He might read more into it than there was.

"I figure you've got young ones who need a *daed,* and I have four daughters who certainly could use a mother's hand. So, since two are better than one, I was wonderin' how you'd feel about marryin' me."

Barbara's mouth fell open. She'd suspected John Frey had marriage on his mind, but she hadn't expected him to be quite so direct. This proposal, if you could call it that, was much too sudden and abrupt. They hadn't courted or even done anything of a social nature together.

"Your silence makes me wonder if you find the idea

of marriage to me objectionable." His forehead wrinkled. "Is it the thought of bein' a bishop's wife that bothers you, or is it our age difference?"

Barbara twisted her hands in her lap. How could she put her feelings into words and not sound as if she were being too particular or unappreciative of his offer? "There is a good fifteen years between us," she admitted, "though I know many folks who've married people much older or younger, and things worked out fine."

His lips turned upward. "That's how I see it, too."

"As far as bein' a bishop's wife, that's not reason enough to keep someone from marryin' another, either."

He jumped up and moved quickly to her side. "Does that mean you'll marry me?"

Barbara cringed. She was making a mess of things and had to fix it before she ended up engaged to this man for whom she felt nothing but respect as her bishop. "I'm not ready to commit to marriage again," she said. "And if I should ever marry, I would want it to be for love, not merely for the sake of convenience."

A pained expression crossed his face, and she knew she had hurt his feelings.

"What you're sayin' is, you don't find me appealing, isn't that right?" The poor man looked as if he'd taken a whiff of apple cider vinegar.

"That's not it at all." Barbara sucked in her lower lip. "It's just that I'm not over the loss of my David yet, and it wouldn't seem right for me to take another husband until the pain subsides."

The bishop paced the length of the porch several times. After a few minutes, he stopped and turned to face her again. "Both of us will always have love in our hearts for the ones we married in our youth. But that shouldn't stop us from startin' a new relationship." He grunted. "Fact is, marryin' again might help heal the pain."

Even if the bishop was right, Barbara didn't want or need a husband right now. She had her hands full making sure her business didn't fail. "I truly do appreciate the offer, John, but—"

He held up one hand, and his jaw clenched and unclenched so fast she worried he might crack a tooth. "You don't have to give me your answer this minute. Just promise you'll think on it, okay?"

Not wishing to hurt the man's feelings, Barbara nodded.

"I'll give you a few more months to make up your mind."

"I . . . uh . . . appreciate that," she mumbled.

He started for the stairs but turned back around and handed her his empty glass. "Just so you know—I won't wait forever."

"No, no, I wouldn't expect you to."

He gave her a quick nod and strode to his buggy.

Barbara headed for the barn. It was time to get her boys inside for lunch. After that, she was determined to do a little work in the harness shop, no matter how drained she felt at the moment.

• • •

Paul glanced at the clock on the far wall. It was almost one, and he'd just finished eating his lunch. His mom had outdone herself that morning when she packed him a container of leftover meatloaf, some potato salad, and tasty baked beans. The food had gone down a lot better than two hunks of bread with a slice of ham sandwiched between, which was what she usually fixed for him.

As he slipped his lunch pail under the counter, Paul thought about the day he'd been invited to join Barbara and her boys for the noon meal. It had been a simple fare, just soup and rolls, but he'd enjoyed it immensely. While the food was good, it wasn't the only thing he had taken pleasure in. Paul liked being around Barbara and her sons. Everyone but Aaron, that is. He wasn't sure he and the boy would ever see eye to eye, but he hoped they could at least come to an understanding, especially if Aaron continued to help in the harness shop during the summer months.

Paul grabbed a piece of leather and was preparing to cut it into a smaller length when the shop door opened. Barbara and Aaron stepped into the room, and his heartbeat quickened. Every time he was around the woman, he felt more drawn to her, and that scared him.

"We thought we'd help out for a few hours," Barbara said. "That is, if you don't mind."

He shook his head. "Don't mind a'tall."

"Anything in particular you're needing help with?" she asked.

He nodded toward the back of the shop. "Your *daed*'s trimming the edges of some leather right now. When he's done, those will need to be dyed."

Barbara's forehead creased. "More black hands for Aaron?"

Paul shrugged. "Maybe you can show him a better way or find some rubber gloves."

Barbara smiled. "I think I may have a pair somewhere that will fit him." She moved away, and Aaron followed.

Paul went back to work on the leather strap he was planning to cut. A short time later, Barbara returned.

"I think Aaron can manage on his own now, so I'm available to help with whatever else needs to be done."

Paul thought a moment. He didn't want her doing anything too strenuous, yet he knew she wanted to feel needed. "How about pressing some grooves into the edges of the straps that have been cut and dyed?"

Barbara nodded. "I can do that. Haven't worked the pressing machine in some time, but it should feel good to get back at it."

Paul watched as she moved to the machine and took up her work. He could see by the smile on her face that she loved working in the harness shop. *And who am I to say otherwise? Just because I don't think this is the kind of work a woman should do, that doesn't mean it's not right for Barbara. Besides, the sooner she gets back to work full time, the sooner I can head for Pennsylvania.*

Paul shook his head. Who was he kidding? He wasn't in a big hurry to return to his cousin's harness shop. He liked it here and wished he could stay. He forced his gaze away from Barbara and onto the job at hand. This kind of thinking was dangerous. Yep, downright precarious.

Barbara straightened with a weary sigh, easing the kinks out of her back. She'd only been working at the pressing machine an hour, and already she felt as if the strength had been drained from her body. *Maybe I wasn't ready to come back yet, not even for a short time.* Tears flooded her eyes and she willed them away. She loved being here in the shop, where the subtle smell of leather mixed with the tangy aroma of linseed and neat's-foot oil. *Just take it slow,* she told herself. *If you work a few hours each week, soon you'll be up to workin' full time again.*

"You okay, daughter?"

Barbara whirled around. She hadn't realized her father had come up behind her. "I'm a bit tired," she admitted. "Guess maybe I should call it a day."

He nodded soberly. "I should think so. You're paler than a bucket of fresh milk. And look at your hands; they're shakin'."

Barbara clasped her fingers tightly together, hoping the action might take away the jittery feeling.

"I can't believe you're even out here today," he said

with a frown. "You oughta be up at the house, takin' care of that new *boppli* of yours."

Barbara's cheeks warmed. "Dad, I'm a grown woman, and I know my limitations. Mom's watchin' Joseph, Zachary, and Davey, and if the *boppli* needs me, she said she would send Joseph straightaway." Barbara's voice quavered, but she hoped her father wouldn't notice.

Paul stepped up beside them. "Everything all right?"

Barbara opened her mouth to respond, but her father cut her off. "She's not ready for this yet. Just look at the way she's tremblin'."

Paul frowned. "I should have been watching closer. Sorry about that, Samuel."

Barbara stomped her foot. "I am not a little girl who needs to be pampered. No one has to watch me or tell me when I should quit workin'."

The men just stood there, apparently dumbfounded by her outburst.

"Your *daed*'s right about how tired you look," Paul finally said. "But if you want to continue working, it's your right to do so. After all, this is your shop, and you're the boss."

Not this again, Barbara fumed. *Why does he feel the need to keep reminding me that I'm the boss?*

She drew in a deep breath. "Actually, I should check on the baby. So if I'm not needed for anything else, I think I'll go on up to the house."

"I'm sure we can manage," Paul said, glancing at Barbara's father.

"*Jah,* with Aaron's help, we'll do fine."

"All right, then." Barbara headed for the door. She was about to open it when Paul tapped her on the shoulder. "Can I speak with you a minute, outside?"

Barbara nodded.

When they were out of the shop, she asked, "What is it?"

A thick silence followed. Paul stared at the ground and pushed the toe of his boot around, making little circles in the dirt. Barbara listened to the soft swooshing sound and wondered when or if he was going to tell her what was on his mind.

"I was wondering if you've thought any more about Saturday."

"Saturday?"

"*Jah,* my invitation to take you and the boys to the pond for a picnic and to do some fishing."

Barbara slid her tongue across her lower lip as she contemplated the idea. She hated to disappoint the boys, and she didn't want to send the three oldest ones with Paul while she stayed home with the baby. What if one of them fell in the water and he didn't see them in time? A lot could happen with three little boys, and she needed to be there to watch out for them.

"It will be a lot of fun," he prompted.

"*Jah,* okay. We'll go."

He grinned at her. "That's great. I'll check with my older brother and see if he has a pole I can borrow."

Barbara thought about loaning him David's pole, but that idea didn't sit well with her. It wouldn't seem right to see someone else using her husband's fishing rod. "See you Saturday if not before," she said with a nod.

He turned back to the shop. "You can count on it."

eleven

Barbara didn't go out to the harness shop the rest of the week. She simply didn't feel up to it. She was, however, looking forward to taking the boys to the pond with Paul on Saturday afternoon.

When the day came, she packed a picnic lunch, which they would eat at suppertime. Paul had promised to come by the house as soon as he closed the harness shop at three.

When she glanced at the kitchen clock, a sense of apprehension crept up her spine. Should she have accepted Paul's invitation? Was she ready for a day of fun and relaxation? She'd gone to bed early the night before and had even taken a short nap with the baby and Zachary right after lunch. Maybe the fresh air and sunshine would do her some good. The boys would enjoy it, she was certain of that much.

She opened the back door and spotted Aaron and Joseph. They were sitting on the porch step with a jar of ladybugs they'd caught. "You two need to go out to the barn and look for your fishing poles," she said.

Joseph set his jar on the porch and jumped up, but Aaron just sat there.

"Aaron, did you hear what I said?"

"I don't wanna go fishin' today."

"Why not? You love to fish."

"Only with Grandpa . . . and Papa when he was alive." Aaron's shoulders shook, which let Barbara know he was struggling not to cry.

She took a seat on the step beside him. "Grandpa's busy today, and Paul was nice enough to invite us. Don't you think you should go?"

He shook his head.

"It might hurt Paul's feelings if you don't come."

"I don't care."

"But you can't stay home alone."

"I can go over to Grandma's."

She took hold of his hand. "You'd rather spend the day with her than at the pond fishing?"

He nodded soberly.

Barbara blew out her breath in a weary sigh. "All right, then. If it's okay with Grandma, you can stay at their place."

Paul couldn't remember the last time he'd been this excited about going fishing. Was it the anticipation of catching a mess of catfish that had him so hyped, or was it the idea of spending time with Barbara and her boys? *A little of both,* he admitted as he turned the wick down on the kerosene lantern above his workbench.

He reached under the bench and grabbed the fishing pole his brother Monroe had loaned him, then headed out the door.

When he arrived at Barbara's house, Paul discovered Zachary and Joseph sitting on the porch step, each with a small fishing pole in his hand. He grinned at their enthusiasm. *Must like fishing as much as I do.* Even Zachary, barely old enough to hold a pole, was smiling from ear to ear.

"We've been waitin' for you," Joseph said eagerly. "Want me to call Mama?"

Paul stepped onto the porch. "Sure, if you don't mind."

"Don't mind a'tall." Joseph jumped up, leaned his pole against the porch railing, and scurried into the house. A few minutes later, he returned carrying a wicker picnic basket. Barbara followed, holding the baby.

"Sure you don't mind me bringin' little David along?" she asked. "I just fed him, so he could be left with my *mamm* for a few hours."

Paul shook his head. "I think he'll be fine under the makeshift tent I've got stashed in my buggy. Besides, if you bring the *boppli* along, we won't have to hurry back if the fish are biting."

She smiled. "That's true."

Paul took the picnic basket from Joseph, then glanced around. "Say, where's Aaron? Does he know it's time to go?"

"He ain't comin'," Joseph announced.

Paul glanced at Barbara.

"He said he'd rather stay with his *grossmudder* today," she said.

Paul shrugged and started for the buggy. If Aaron didn't want to go, there wasn't much he could do about it. The boy obviously didn't care to spend the day with him. Either that, or Aaron had no interest in fishing.

Forcing the negative thoughts aside, Paul loaded the two boys into the backseat. Barbara and the baby sat up front with him.

As they pulled out of the yard, Paul caught a glimpse of Aaron heading for the barn. Barbara waved, but the boy didn't even look their way.

"Aaron's missin' his *daed,*" she said as though she could read Paul's mind.

He nodded. "I figured as much."

"He remembers when they went fishing together, and I guess going to the pond today would be too painful."

"He'll come around in time." Even as the words slipped off his tongue, Paul wondered if they would ever come true. Aaron might not ever get over his father's death. And there was a good chance the child would never take a liking to Paul.

"I hope you're right." Barbara cuddled the baby. "At least Aaron will have some memories of his *daed,* which is more than this little guy will." She glanced behind her. "For that matter, Zachary probably won't remember David. I'm not even sure about Joseph."

Paul wished there was something he could say or do to ease the pain he saw on Barbara's face. It wasn't fair that she had to bear the loss of her husband and try to raise four boys on her own. It didn't seem right for Margaret, his brother's widow, to go through life on her own, either. At least her four children were grown, and two were out on their own already.

Paul's thoughts went to John Frey. Had the man considered Margaret as a candidate for marriage? Maybe not, since she'd only been a widow for a few weeks. It didn't seem proper for the bishop to court a newly widowed woman.

When Barbara's baby made a gurgling sound, Paul set his thoughts aside. With a feeling of concern, he glanced over at her. "Is he doing okay?"

She nodded. "I think he's enjoyin' the ride."

Paul looked over his shoulder. "The boys in the back must be, too. They're fast asleep."

Barbara chuckled. "I'm guessin' as soon as we pull up to the pond they'll be wide awake and rarin' to go."

"Sure hope the fish are biting today," he said. "Wouldn't want to disappoint the *kinner.*"

"Zachary's not really old enough to fish yet, so I doubt he'd care if they weren't bitin'."

"Joseph might, though."

"Maybe. But he's so taken with you, he'd probably be happy just sittin' on the grass by your side."

"Sure don't know why. I've never been that comfortable with little ones, and I think most of them feel the same way about me."

Barbara reached over and touched his arm. "I believe Joseph sees somethin' you don't."

The feel of her slender fingers on his bare skin made

Paul's arm tingle. He inhaled deeply, searching for something else to talk about. "We're getting close to the pond. I can smell it," he said as she pulled her hand away.

"*Jah.*"

A short time later, they pulled into a grassy spot. Paul had no sooner secured the horse to a tree than the boys woke up and clambered out of the buggy "Here, let me help you down," Paul said, offering Barbara his hand.

She leaned forward and gave him the baby. "If you'll take Davey, I can get out of the buggy a little easier."

Reluctantly, Paul took the infant. He'd never held a *boppli* this young before and wasn't sure if he was doing it right. He positioned the child so he was lying against his shoulder, then he patted the little fellow's back, feeling more awkward by the minute.

As soon as Barbara stepped down, she took her son. Paul felt a sense of relief. He'd seen many fathers hold their babies and look perfectly comfortable, but he doubted he ever would, even if he should become a *daed* himself someday.

Paul reached under the front seat and grabbed an old quilt. He handed it to Barbara. "If you and the boys want to get settled, I'll get the rest of the stuff unloaded."

"Joseph can help," she said.

Paul nodded toward the shoreline. The boys were already romping back and forth, throwing rocks into the water. "Let them play. I can manage."

"All right." Barbara headed for a grassy area not far from the water.

In short order, Paul had a little tent set up for the baby and placed the carriage under it. Barbara put the infant inside and draped a piece of netting over the sides. After Paul got the boys' fishing poles ready, he baited Barbara's hook and handed her the pole.

"Thanks." She placed it on the ground, pulled her skirt around her legs, and took a seat on the grass. "I'm not used to having someone wait on me."

He grinned and sat next to her, noticing that she looked more rested today. "Feels kind of nice to be doing this."

She looked away shyly. Did she think he was being too forward?

She leaned toward the pond and cupped her hands around her mouth. "Joseph, Paul has your poles ready. Bring Zachary over here and let's do some fishin'."

The boys came running, and soon all four of them had their lines in the water. The sound of the children's laughter rippled over Paul like a bubbling brook. As the sun beat down on their heads, the birds overhead sang a joyous tune. Savoring the moment, Paul closed his eyes and allowed himself to drift into a fanciful daydream in which he was married to Barbara, and her boys were his own.

Barbara couldn't get over how comfortable she felt with Paul. She fixed her gaze on him, watching his every move. Her heart hammered as she was hurled into a whirlwind of conflicting emotions. It was almost as if they were . . .

She shook her head. She couldn't allow herself the luxury of becoming attached to Paul. She had a business to run, not to mention four boys to raise. There wasn't time for romantic notions or even a close friendship with someone who'd be leaving Webster County soon.

Barbara chewed on her lower lip as she continued to mull things over. *Even if I did feel free to begin a relationship with Paul, and even if I knew he wanted one, as well, he's never been married I'm sure he wouldn't want to take on the responsibility of raising another man's children, especially when one of them doesn't seem to like him.* Besides, she barely knew Paul and had no right to think of him in any way other than as her temporary employee.

"I've got a bite!" Joseph hollered. "I think it's a big one!"

Barbara was glad for the interruption to her ridiculous thoughts.

"Hold tight," Paul instructed as he sprang to his feet. "Would ya help me reel him in?"

He grabbed Joseph's pole and held it steady.

"Don't let him get away," the child panted.

Paul took over for Joseph. After several great tugs, a nice big catfish lay flopping at the boy's feet.

Zachary squealed and jumped up and down. *"Fisch! Fisch!"*

Barbara laughed. It felt *wunderbaar* to see her boys

having such a good time. Paul was as enthusiastic as both of them as he pointed to Joseph's trophy. *"Es bescht,"* he said with a wide grin.

Joseph nodded. *"Jah,* the best."

Paul removed the hook, then placed the catfish in a bucket of water.

For the next hour they continued to fish. By the end of the afternoon, each of them, including Zachary, had caught at least one fish. The boys took turns vying for Paul's attention, plopping down beside him and some-times even crawling into his lap.

After awhile the baby woke up and started to howl.

Zachary and Joseph covered their ears. "Make him quit, Mama," they pleaded in unison.

"There's only one way to stop his crying," Barbara said. "I'll need to feed him."

Feeling the heat of a blush cover her cheeks, she looked over at Paul. "Mind if I take the *boppli* to your buggy and nurse him?"

Paul nodded, and she noticed his face was red, too. "Sure, go ahead. When you're done we can eat our picnic supper."

Half an hour later, the baby was fed and back in his carriage, and Barbara had the contents of their picnic basket spread on the blanket. They bowed for silent prayer, then dug into the fried chicken, baked beans, carrot sticks, and rolls she'd brought for their meal. Noah had stopped by the harness shop that morning and given Paul a batch of peanut butter cookies, so he'd furnished the dessert.

"Everything tastes great," Paul said. "Especially the chicken."

"It's a recipe my *mamm* and her *mamm* used to make," she said with a smile. "I call it Webster County Fried Chicken."

When Barbara handed Paul a glass of lemonade, her fingers brushed his. The touch of his hand did funny things to her insides, and a strange warmth crept through her body. She hadn't felt this giddy since her courting days with David. It was more than a bit disconcerting.

Paul smiled. *"Danki."*

She returned his smile, realizing that despite her best intentions, a special kind of friendship was taking root in her heart. There didn't have to be love or romance for her to enjoy the company of a man—especially this man, for whom she was sure there could never be anything more than friendship.

twelve

Paul was glad to have an off-Sunday when there would be no church. It wasn't that he disliked the preaching, songs, or reading of the scriptures. He just wanted some time alone, without a crowd of people around him. After yesterday's trip to the pond, he needed to think and pray. He'd had a good time with Barbara and her boys. *Too good, maybe,* Paul reflected as he headed for his folks' barn right after breakfast. Since he couldn't do any work that wasn't absolutely necessary on this day of rest, he decided a little get-away might do him some good.

As soon as Paul entered the rustic building, he took a seat on a bale of straw in one corner of the room. He'd come here countless times when he was a boy, and it had always been a good place to think and pray.

"Heavenly Father, I don't know why I'm so drawn to Barbara. Mom told me how hard Barbara grieved when David was killed, and I have an inkling she might still be grieving her loss." A vision of Barbara's pretty face popped into his head. "Despite my attraction to her, Lord, I know it's not likely she'd ever be interested in me. She's got the bishop after her, and I suspect she's considered marrying him."

The barn door creaked, and Paul's eyes snapped open.

"Paul?"

"Yeah, Pop, over here."

His dad removed his straw hat, revealing a thick crop of nearly gray hair, then hung it on a nail. "Whatcha doin' in here?"

"Just sitting, thinking, and praying."

"Always did like to hide out in the barn, didn't ya?"

"*Jah.*"

"I'd like to talk to you for a minute, if you're done prayin'."

"Sure, Pop, what's up?"

His dad leaned against one of the wooden beams as he studied Paul. "Your brothers and me could use some help in the fields next week. We were hopin' we could count on you."

Paul shifted uneasily on the bale of hay. "Sorry, but I can't."

"Why not?"

Paul blew out an exasperated breath. "I can't leave Barbara in the lurch."

Pop squinted his pale blue eyes. "She ain't back to work yet?"

Paul shook his head.

"When will she be?"

He shrugged. "Don't rightly know. She tried working a few hours one day last week, but I think it took its toll on her."

Pop crossed his arms. "Your *mamm* tells me Barbara and a couple of her *kinner* went fishin' with you yesterday afternoon. Doesn't sound to me like she's so weak."

Paul felt his defenses rise and his face heat up. "Sitting on a grassy bank with a fishing pole is relaxing. Not hard work like the things we do in the harness shop."

His father's face contorted. "*Jah,* well, it makes me wonder if there ain't more goin' on with you and Barbara than just you workin' for her."

Paul clenched his fists. His *daed* had no right to be saying such things, but he didn't want to respond disrespectfully. There had been too many harsh words between him and Pop in the past.

"There's nothing going on between me and Barbara," he said slowly. "I promised to help her out 'til she's back on her feet, and I aim to do just that."

Pop grunted. "And then what?"

"Then I'll be on my way back to Lancaster County to work in Abe's harness shop."

"Didn't figure it would be any different." Pop grabbed his straw hat off the nail, pushed it onto his head, and stalked out of the barn, letting the door slam shut behind him.

Paul shook his head. "Guess some things will never change."

Barbara stood on the front porch of her house, leaning against the rail. She tried to keep her focus on her three boys, who were playing in the yard. But her thoughts kept taking her back to the pond, where she'd had such a good time with Paul. Yesterday he had shown a side of himself she hadn't known existed. Usually serious and strictly business, Paul had joked with her, frolicked with Zachary and Joseph, and seemed genuinely relaxed. He'd even commented on how much the baby was growing and said he was a cute little guy. As long as they stayed away from the topic of the harness shop, Barbara and Paul got along quite well.

"Mama, Aaron's bein' mean."

Barbara whirled around at the sound of Joseph's voice. "What's the problem, son?" she asked, leaning over and wiping away the tears glistening on Joseph's cheeks.

"He says Paul's tryin' to be our new papa."

Barbara's mouth dropped open. "Where did he get such a notion?"

"I was tellin' him how much fun we had at the pond yesterday, and how Paul said he wished he had a son like me." Joseph's lower lip quivered. "Aaron said Paul was just tryin' to butter me up. He said that Paul's a mean man."

"And what has Paul done to make Aaron think he's mean?"

Joseph sniffed. "He says Paul's always giving him crummy jobs to do in the harness shop."

Barbara pursed her lips. She knew Paul had given Aaron menial jobs to do. But he was only eight and a half years old—too young to do anything complicated or anything that required heavy lifting. She also knew the child wanted to help in the shop and figured he would appreciate any job, no matter how small. Fact was, Aaron had never complained when his *daed* gave him easy chores to do. Barbara suspected Aaron's dislike of Paul had more to do with him not wanting anyone to take his father's place than it did with the jobs that had been required of him.

She tousled Joseph's curly blond hair and gave him a hug. "I'll speak to Aaron about his attitude. In the meantime, why don't you get Zachary and take him inside? There's a jar of chocolate chip cookies on the cupboard. Grandma made them yesterday. You two can have some with a glass of milk if you like."

Joseph smiled, and his blue eyes brightened. "Okay." He scampered off the porch.

Barbara glanced across the yard. Aaron was seated on the swing hanging from the maple tree, but he wasn't swinging at the moment. He just sat there, kicking at a clump of grass with his bare toes.

Lord, please give me the right words, Barbara prayed as she headed for the swing.

Aaron looked up when she approached. "I suppose that tattletale Joseph told you we was arguin' about Paul Hilty," he said with a lift of his chin.

She nodded. "Did you tell your brother that Paul was mean and tryin' to butter him up?"

He nodded. "Yep, and I meant it, too."

"That wasn't nice, and it's not even true."

He grunted. "You haven't seen the way that guy treats me in the harness shop—like I'm stupid or somethin'."

"Are the jobs Paul has given you any different from the ones you did for your *daed?*"

He hung his head. "Not really, but—"

"Then why do you think Paul's treating you differently?"

His only response was a slight shrug.

"He's giving you jobs you're able to do. Keep doing them well, and I'm sure Paul will give you other jobs as he sees that you're capable of doing them."

Aaron made no reply, just stared straight ahead.

"You need to give Paul a chance to get to know you better," Barbara said softly. "Maybe you should have gone fishing with us. Then you'd have seen for yourself that he's not mean at all."

"*Humph!* All Joseph's been talkin' about since Saturday is that dumb old fishin' trip and how much fun he had with Paul." Aaron wrinkled his nose. "He favors my younger brothers, that's for certain sure."

Barbara knelt on the ground and gently touched Aaron's knee. "That's not true, son. Paul has reached out to Joseph and Zachary, but that's because they've reached out to him. If you would give the man half a chance, I'm sure you and he could become friends, too."

Aaron started pumping the swing. "I don't care if he takes 'em fishin' every day of the week. I'm never gonna like him!"

Barbara wanted to say more, but the words wouldn't come. It wasn't likely anything she had to say would change Aaron's mind anyway. That would have to come from Paul, and since he wouldn't be staying around Webster County much longer, she doubted there could be a resolution. All the more reason she had to get back to work as soon as possible. If Aaron were helping her instead of Paul, she was sure he'd be more agreeable.

"Your brothers are havin' cookies and milk up at the house," she said, turning away. "If you've a mind to join them, I'm sure there's plenty left."

Aaron kept swinging but remained silent. Barbara walked away with a sick feeling in the pit of her stomach. Her oldest boy was becoming more belligerent all the time. If he didn't come to grips with his father's death soon, she wondered if he would carry this resentment into his adult life. She had to find some way to help him. Maybe if she spoke to her *daed*, he could get through to Aaron.

Barbara headed for the house. When she stepped into the kitchen, she was greeted with a mess. Joseph and Zachary sat at the table with chocolate all over their faces and crumbs covering their light blue cotton shirts. The cookie jar was nearly empty, and a bottle of milk sat beside it, with nothing left inside. The milk was all on the floor.

"What happened here?" Barbara screeched. "Just look at the disaster you two have caused!"

Joseph gave her a sheepish look. Zachary continued to munch on the cookie he held in his hand.

"Sorry, Mama," Joseph said. "The bottle slipped out of my hands and landed on the floor."

Barbara blew out her breath and grabbed a sponge from the kitchen sink. So much for the quiet Sunday morning she'd hoped to have. First Aaron's impossible attitude, and now this!

Just then the baby started to howl from the next room, where she'd put him down for a nap in the portable crib.

"The *boppli*'s awake," Joseph announced.

"I can hear him." Barbara tossed the sponge onto the kitchen table. "Here, Joseph. Please get things cleaned up while I tend to Davey." She marched out of the room before he had a chance to respond. Tomorrow she would go to work in the harness shop, no matter how tired she felt. At least then there might be some sense of normalcy in her life again.

thirteen

For the next several weeks, Barbara forced herself to get out of bed early, feed the boys, and send them to her folks' house every other day. With a renewed sense of determination, she went to work in the harness shop, taking breaks only for lunch and to feed the baby. Twice a week, on the days her father went to Springfield for physical therapy, she took Aaron along so he could help, too. Dad's hands had become increasingly stiffer, but the therapy and wax treatments seemed to help.

At Barbara's request, her father had spoken to Aaron about his attitude. The boy wouldn't open up to his grandpa, but he seemed a little more compliant while working at the shop after that. Then again, Barbara suspected it was because she was there, too.

This morning, as she cleared the breakfast table, Barbara noticed for the first time in many weeks that her energy level was actually up. *Maybe it's because my appetite's back,* she mused. *Or it could have to do with the fact that I'm back doing what I love best— making and repairing leather items. Maybe I can start workin' full time soon.*

She placed a stack of dishes in the sink and ran water over them. It wasn't easy being a full-time mother and running a business, but she enjoyed the work, and it did support her family.

"I'm ready to go when you are, Mama."

Barbara turned at the sound of Aaron's voice. "I've

still got to feed the *boppli*. Why don't you head out to the shop? Zachary and Joseph are already at Grandma's, so I'll be along shortly."

Aaron's dark brows drew together. "I'd rather wait for you."

"But Paul might need you for something."

Aaron shifted his weight from one foot to the other. "Do I have to go now?"

She nodded.

"All right." Aaron turned toward the door. "Don't be too long, okay?" he called over his shoulder.

"If your wee brother cooperates, I shouldn't be more than half an hour."

Aaron's shoulders were slumped as he headed out the door.

"I love you, Aaron," Barbara called.

"*Naemlich da*—I love you."

The door clicked shut, and Barbara headed into the next room to get the baby. She prayed things would go all right between Aaron and Paul today.

Paul had just entered the back room and started to look over an old saddle, brought in yesterday by an English man, when he heard the front door of the shop open.

"I'm back here, Barbara," he called.

A few seconds later, Aaron came into the room. "It's only me," he said.

"*Gude mariye,*" Paul responded, hoping the greeting would wipe the scowl off the boy's face.

"Mornin'," Aaron mumbled.

"Where's your *mamm?*"

"Had to feed the baby. Said she'd be here soon."

Paul reached for a clean rag and handed it to Aaron. "Why don't you rub this saddle down with oil while I take care of a few other things?"

Aaron responded with a muffled grunt, but he did take the rag.

"If you need me, I'll be up front at my desk, looking over some work orders."

"It ain't your desk," Aaron muttered. "It belonged to my *daed.*"

The child's ears turned bright pink, a good indication that he was angry. Paul blew out an exasperated breath. Wouldn't the boy ever lower his defenses?

"I know it's not my desk," Paul said. "It was a figure of speech."

No reply.

Paul shrugged and left the room. *Sure hope Barbara gets here soon.*

Forty-five minutes later, Barbara showed up. "Sorry I'm late," she said breathlessly. "I got the *boppli* fed okay, but then he wouldn't burp."

"No problem," Paul replied, barely looking up from the papers on the desk.

"Everything going okay?"

"Yep."

"What have you got Aaron doin'?"

"Oiling a saddle in the other room." Paul craned his neckin that direction. "Sure is taking him awhile to get it done."

"Maybe he finished and found something else to do."

"Didn't give him any other chores."

"Want me to check on him?" Barbara asked.

"Sure."

She took a step toward the back room but turned around and leaned over the desk. "Any new work orders I should know about?"

Paul glanced down at the stack lying before him. When he brought his head up again, it connected with Barbara's.

"Ouch!" they said in unison.

"Sorry." Paul rubbed his forehead. "You okay?"

She placed her fingers against her head. "Don't feel a lump anywhere."

"That's *gut*."

She glanced at him with an anxious expression. Then she reached out and touched his forehead. "You, on the other hand, do have a little bump."

Her fingers felt cool. Paul's heart pounded when he noticed the tender look in her eyes. An unexpected flame ignited in his chest, and he fought against the sudden urge to kiss her. "I . . . uh . . . it's nothing to worry about."

Barbara pulled her hand away, but her touch lingered in his mind. His arms ached to hold her. His lips yearned for the touch of hers. This wasn't good. Not good at all.

Paul grabbed a work order off the top of the pile. "This one's the most recent," he said, handing the piece of paper to Barbara and hoping his trembling hands wouldn't give him away.

She pursed her lips as she studied it. "Is this the saddle Aaron's workin' on?"

He nodded, afraid if he spoke, his voice might reveal the emotions he struggled so hard to control.

Her eyebrows drew together. "But this says Harold Shaw wants the saddle repaired, not oiled or cleaned. Haven't you got Aaron doing something completely unnecessary?"

Paul sat up straight as the feelings of tenderness he'd had for Barbara only moments ago dissolved like a block of ice left sitting in the sun. What right did she have to question him like this? Didn't the woman realize it was good business to clean and oil a saddle that had been brought in for repair? He opened his mouth to say so, but she spoke first.

"David always asked the customers if they wanted something cleaned or oiled. If they did, he wrote it on the work order so I would know. If not, then we didn't do it." She blinked a couple of times. "No point doing something not asked for when there's lots of other work to be done."

A muscle in Paul's cheek quivered, and he reached up to massage the spot.

Barbara placed one hand against her hip and stared at him. "Your silence makes me wonder if you disagree with that practice."

He shrugged. "This is your harness shop. Who am I to say anything about the way you do business?"

She tipped her head. "After workin' together these

past few weeks, I think we know each other well enough to be honest. I'd like it if we could express our thoughts and concerns, not clam up or become defensive."

He pushed the chair away from the desk and stood. "I'd say you've expressed your thoughts clear enough for the both of us."

When he started to walk away, she stepped in front of him. "I think we need to talk about this."

"Ain't much to be said." He grunted. "You see things one way, and I see them another. You're the boss here. I'm just helping out 'til you're back working full time."

"I would like to hear your reason for oiling the saddle without Harold having asked."

Paul reached up to rub his forehead. That bump from their heads colliding hurt more than he realized. Either that or he was getting a headache caused by stress.

"Paul?"

"Yeah?"

"Are you gonna share your thoughts on this or not?"

"I don't see how it'll do much good."

"Please."

He motioned for her to sit down. When she complied, he leaned over and pointed to the stack of work orders. "If you'll look through these, you'll see some of them are from customers who have returned more than once since I started working here."

"And?"

"After their first order, they found other things for me to do. Things they said they'd originally planned to do themselves."

She looked at him over her shoulder. "Then why didn't they?"

"Some said I had done such a thorough job on their previous order, they decided to bring in a second or third item."

She turned in her chair and nodded slowly. "I see what you mean."

"My cousin Abe taught me that doing a little something extra for a customer makes for good business."

"Guess you're right. I should have realized that." Barbara's dark eyes took on a faraway look. "I'm sure David tried to please our customers. But sometimes, when we got real busy, he might not have thought to do the little extra things."

Paul smiled, feeling somewhat better now. "I'm sure David was good at his job. He and you made this business succeed."

She returned his smile. *"Danki."*

Paul touched her shoulder. "Barbara, I—"

His words were cut off when the front door opened, and in walked Bishop John Frey.

"Gude mariye, John," Barbara said. "What brings you by the harness shop?"

Paul stepped aside as the bishop walked up to the desk and offered her a wide smile. "Came to see about gettin' a new bridle for one of my drivin' horses." He

119

held out the paper sack he had in his hand. "Also wanted to give you this."

Barbara took the sack and peered inside at a loaf of bread with a very dark crust. It appeared to be overly baked.

"My oldest daughter made it," John said with a crooked grin. "Figured with you back workin' again, you probably wouldn't have much time for bakin' these days."

"I'm managing with Mom's help, but I appreciate the gesture. Tell your daughter I said thanks."

Paul cleared his throat, and she turned toward him.

"Why don't you check on Aaron?" she suggested.

"You're the boss." He gave the bishop a quick nod and headed for the back of the shop.

Barbara set the bread aside, pulled out her order pad, and grabbed a pencil. "Let's see now . . . you said you wanted a new bridle?"

"*Jah,* that's right."

"Shouldn't be a problem." Barbara scrawled the bishop's name at the top of the page and wrote down the order. "You want black or brown?"

"Black. And nothin' fancy added." He puffed out his chest a bit. "Wouldn't do for the bishop to be drivin' around usin' a worldly-looking bridle on his buggy horse."

"No, of course not."

When Barbara finished writing up the order, she tore off the top sheet and handed it to John, placing the carbon copy in the basket with their other orders. "If you'd like to drop by in a few weeks, we'll have the bridle ready for you."

His forehead wrinkled. "I was kind of hopin' to come by sooner than that."

She tapped the tip of the pencil against the desk. "Don't think we can have it ready any sooner."

He grunted. "That's not what I meant."

"Oh?"

"I was plannin' to come callin' on you. Maybe take you and the boys for a drive or on a picnic."

Barbara gulped and tried to keep her composure. If the bishop had heard she'd gone fishing and shared a picnic supper with Paul a few weeks ago, there was no way she could tell him she wasn't up to such an outing yet. Besides, it would be a lie, and her conscience wouldn't let her knowingly tell an untruth.

"How about it, Barbara? Can I come by on Saturday and pick you all up?"

She nibbled on the inside of her cheek, searching for the right words. "Well, I . . . uh . . . appreciate the offer, but—"

"She's made other plans."

Barbara dropped the pencil and whirled around in her chair. Paul stood slightly behind her, off to one side. She opened her mouth to ask what other plans she had for Saturday, but the bishop cut her off.

"Is that so? What kind of plans?"

"She and the boys are going fishing with me," Paul said boldly. The look of determination on his face made Barbara wonder what was going on. He hadn't said a word to her about going fishing again, but the idea did sound appealing, especially if it gave her an excuse to turn down the bishop's invitation.

A warm rush spread through Barbara. She struggled to hide the unexpected pleasure of knowing he was speaking on her behalf.

John took a few steps in Paul's direction and scowled at him. "I hear from your *daed* that you're plannin' to return to Pennsylvania soon."

Paul shrugged. "When Barbara doesn't need me anymore."

The bishop turned his gaze on Barbara. "How long will that be?"

She felt her face heat up. "Really, Bishop Frey, I don't think—"

"I've asked ya to call me John."

Before Barbara could respond, Paul jumped in. "We haven't set a date for my leaving, but since you're so interested, I'll be sure to let you know when it's time for me to go."

Barbara couldn't believe Paul's boldness or the way his eyes flashed when he spoke to John. What was he thinking, speaking to their bishop that way? *Of course, he's not Paul's bishop,* she reasoned. *Paul lives in Pennsylvania and has his own bishop there.*

John shook his finger in Paul's face. "I'll have you know, I've asked Barbara to be my wife. Has she told ya that?"

A vein on the side of Paul's neck bulged. Violence went against their teachings, and yet Barbara worried he might be about to punch the bishop right in the nose.

"Mama, are you gonna marry the bishop?"

Barbara whirled around. She hadn't realized Aaron had come onto the scene.

She reached for her son's hand. "I've made no promises to marry anyone. Only said I'd think on it."

Aaron looked at the bishop. "My *mamm* don't need another husband. She's got me to help out." Then he looked at Paul. "Someday this harness shop will be mine, and then nobody can tell me what to do!" Aaron rushed out the door. Barbara just sat there, too stunned to say a word.

fourteen

Barbara couldn't believe she had let Paul talk her into going fishing again, yet here they were, heading for the pond—this time with all four boys in tow. Aaron had put up a fuss, but Barbara held firm, saying the outing would be good for him. The boys sat in the backseat, and she and the baby were up front with Paul, same as last time. She hoped today would be as pleasant as their other fishing date had been.

It's strange, Barbara thought as she cast a sidelong glance at Paul. *We get along fine at certain times, and other times we're at odds with each other.*

She wished she understood what attracted her to him. *Other than our love for harness-making and our commitment to God, we're as different as north is from south. 'Course, we do both enjoy fishing.*

"Sure is a nice day," Paul said, breaking into her thoughts.

She nodded. "I love it here in Webster County, especially the warm days of summer."

He grunted. "I'm not really partial to hot, muggy weather."

"Doesn't it get humid in Pennsylvania?"

"*Jah.*"

"But you still like it there?"

"I like my job."

"Wasn't it hard to leave your family and friends and move so far away?" she questioned.

"*Jah,* it was. But I didn't want to farm. I wanted to work in a harness shop. You and David owned the shop here, and I didn't think there'd be a need for a second one in our small community." He glanced over at her. "So going to Pennsylvania to help my cousin was the only way I could do what I wanted."

Barbara could see by the wistful expression on Paul's face that he would have preferred to open a harness shop here rather than move to Pennsylvania. A sense of guilt stabbed her, but she realized it wasn't her fault Paul had chosen to move. If he'd wanted to work in a harness shop that badly, he could have talked to David about working for him. Maybe Barbara never would have become interested in working with leather if her husband had hired a helper.

"Did you ever talk to David about goin' to work for him?" she asked.

"By the time I figured out what I wanted to do, you

were already his partner, and I didn't think he'd need anyone else in the shop."

"He could have used you part-time, whenever I wasn't able to be there."

He shook his head. "Didn't want to work part-time. Pop would have expected me to farm when I wasn't helping David."

She could understand why he felt forced to leave Webster County and find work someplace else. But from the tone of his voice, Barbara sensed there was bitterness in Paul's heart toward his dad.

"Sure hope the fish are biting today," he said. "I'd like to catch me some nice bass this time."

Barbara nodded, glad for the change of subject. "I think my boys would agree." She shifted the sleeping baby in her arms and glanced over her shoulder. Joseph and Zachary were drawing on their tablets. Aaron sat there with his arms folded, looking straight ahead. She hoped once they got to the pond and he saw how much fun the others were having, his attitude would improve.

A few minutes later, Zachary leaned over the seat and tapped his mother on the shoulder. "Mama, I'm hungry."

"We'll eat when we get there." She touched Paul's arm lightly. "Would you mind if we have supper before we fish?"

He chuckled and patted his stomach. "Sounds *gut* to me. I'm always ready for food."

When they pulled into the grassy area by the pond, Barbara noticed another open buggy parked there. She thought she recognized it, and her suspicions were confirmed when she saw Bishop John Frey sitting on a large rock holding a fishing pole.

"What's he doing here?" Paul mumbled. "I'll bet he only came 'cause he knew we were coming."

"It's a free country," Barbara reminded him. "He has as much right to be here as we do."

When Paul came around to help Barbara and the boys down from the buggy, Barbara noticed deep furrows in his forehead. He was obviously not happy about having to share their fishing spot.

"Maybe we should go to the other side of the pond," Paul suggested. "Wouldn't want to scare away any fish the bishop wants to catch."

Before Barbara could reply, her three boys took off on a run, heading straight for the pond.

"Yippee!" Zachary shouted. "We're gonna eat!"

"And fish for some big ol' bass!" Joseph hollered.

Barbara grasped Paul's arm. "So much for not disturbing the bishop."

Paul's skin prickled and turned to gooseflesh under his short-sleeved cotton shirt. Every time he and Barbara made physical contact, his insides turned to mush.

If I had a lick of sense, I'd catch the next bus heading for Pennsylvania and let Barbara marry the old bishop. Paul grimaced. *Of course, she might become the man's wife even if I did stick around.*

"Would you mind holdin' the baby while I get the picnic basket out of the buggy?" Barbara asked.

126

He blinked. "Huh?"

"I said—"

"Yeah, I heard, but don't you think it would be better if I got the basket, and you kept the *boppli* held securely in your arms?"

She grinned at him, and his heart did a little flip-flop. "He won't bite, ya know. Davey has no teeth yet."

Paul's face heated up. He didn't want to admit how uncomfortable it had made him feel the last time he'd held the infant. What if the little guy started to howl or spit up all over him?

"I think you're blushin', Paul Hilty," Barbara said with a playful wink. "A big man like you isn't afraid of a baby, I hope."

Regaining his composure, Paul held out his hands. "Ain't afraid of too much. Leastways, not a little scrap of a guy like Davey."

She chuckled and reached into the buggy to grab a quilt, which she tucked under Paul's arm. "Why don't you ask Aaron to spread this on the grass? You and Davey can have a seat, and I'll be there soon with our picnic supper."

"What about the *boppli*'s carriage?"

"We can get it later."

Feeling like a schoolboy who knew better than to argue with his teacher, Paul did as she asked. When he suggested Aaron put the quilt on the ground, the boy complied, but not without giving Paul a disgruntled look. To make matters worse, he placed the blanket not three feet from where the bishop sat fishing.

"Good day to ya, Paul," John said with a slight nod. "Looks like you've got your hands full."

Paul felt his face flood with warmth again. He hated how easily he blushed. "How's the fishing?" he asked, avoiding the bishop's comment.

"Got myself a couple bass and some catfish." The man nodded toward his cooler sitting nearby. "'Course, with the way Barbara's boys are runnin' around hollerin', it'll be harder to lure the fish."

If the bishop was looking for an apology, or even an offer to move, Paul wasn't about to provide him with one. He was pretty sure the man had come here on purpose, knowing Paul was planning to bring Barbara and her boys fishing. Well, two could play that game. If Bishop Frey wanted to marry Barbara, he'd have to earn the right. Coming here pretending he wanted to fish was a sneaky thing to do, but the man hadn't won Barbara's hand or her heart yet. At least as far as Paul knew, he hadn't.

The baby started to cry, and Paul shifted uneasily on the quilt. *Sure hope Barbara shows up soon, or the bishop will have one more thing to razz me about.*

Paul watched in horror as Zachary picked up a flat rock and pitched it into the pond—right in front of John Frey's fishing line. *Splat*! Drops of water splattered everywhere, some landing on the bishop. A few even made it to the quilt Paul sat on. At least he and the baby hadn't gotten wet.

"Hey, watch what you're doin'!" The bishop's face was red, and a vein on the side of his neck stuck out like a noodle boiling in a pot.

"What's goin' on here?"

Paul cranked his head. Barbara stood nearby, holding the picnic basket.

"Your boy, Zachary, is throwin' rocks into the pond," John said before Paul could open his mouth.

Barbara's brows furrowed. "Is that so, Zachary?"

"He only threw one," Paul said in the boy's defense.

"Yes, and it splashed water all over me." The bishop held up his arm, but there was barely a telltale sign of the water droplets left.

Barbara took a step toward her son. "Zachary, tell Bishop John you're sorry."

The boy's lower lip quivered, and he stared down at the grass. "S—s—sorry, Bishop."

"*Jah,* well, don't let it happen again." The bishop smiled up at Barbara. "It's *gut* to see you. Even though your boy tried to drown me."

She nodded but didn't return his smile. Paul felt a sense of relief.

"Come now, boys," Barbara said, grabbing Zachary's hand. "Let's see about eatin' our supper."

Aaron, Joseph, and Zachary followed her to the quilt, and in short order she had the food set out.

"Yum, this looks good," Joseph said, licking his lips.

"Let us pray, and then we'll eat ourselves full," Paul said, handing Barbara the baby.

She turned to face the bishop, who was watching

them like a hungry cat ready to pounce on its unsuspecting prey. "Would you care to join us, John? That is, if you haven't already eaten."

"Haven't had anything since lunch. I'd be much obliged." John quickly reeled in his line and set the fishing pole aside. Then he joined the group, taking a seat beside Barbara.

Paul gritted his teeth. It didn't surprise him when the bishop accepted her invitation, but did he have to plunk down right beside Barbara, as though he was the one who'd brought her and the boys to the pond?

The bishop cleared his throat. "Shall we pray?"

All heads bowed. When he cleared his throat a second time, they opened their eyes.

"Everything looks mighty good," the older man said as he reached for a piece of Barbara's fried chicken.

"I hope it tastes as good as it looks." Barbara handed the platter to Paul, who took a drumstick. Then he passed it to each of her boys.

"Want me to get the *boppli*'s carriage from the buggy so you can eat with both hands?" Paul asked Barbara.

Barbara nodded. "That would be nice."

Paul set the drumstick on his paper plate and stood. When he returned, he set up the carriage and took the baby from her. After the little guy was settled, he draped the netting across the top and sides of the carriage. He sat back down and was about to reach for his piece of chicken when he noticed Aaron's plate still had most of his food on it.

He tapped the boy on the shoulder. "You haven't eaten very much."

Aaron shrugged. "Ain't all that hungry."

"Well, I sure am," John exclaimed. "Guess a few hours of fishin' gave me a hearty appetite." He chomped down the last hunk of the white meat he'd taken and licked his fingers. "Your *mamm* is one fine cook!" He turned to Barbara. "Got any corn bread or baked beans?"

"As a matter of fact, I do." Barbara handed the man the bowl of baked beans, followed by the basket of corn bread.

"Danki."

"You're welcome."

It was all Paul could do to keep from telling the bishop what he thought. He'd wanted to spend the evening with Barbara and her boys, do a little fishing, and hopefully work on his relationship with Aaron. Instead, he was being forced to sit here and watch the bishop eat the choicest pieces of meat, listen to the man praise Barbara for her cooking skills, and watch him make cow eyes over a woman he cared about deeply. Paul was beginning to wish he'd never suggested this outing.

Guess that's what I get for trying to be one up on John Frey. It's only natural Barbara would be interested in a man like him. The bishop has the respect of those in the community, he plans to stay in Webster County, and he's got the smarts to outwit me.

Paul leaned back on one elbow and took a bite of

chicken. *Might as well make the most of the evening,* he decided. *Because if John has his way, this will probably be the last time I take Barbara and her* kinner *anywhere.*

fifteen

On Sunday morning, Barbara awoke with a headache. Church would be held at her in-laws' today, and as much as she enjoyed visiting with Mavis, she dreaded going. It wasn't merely the constant pounding in her head that made her want to stay home in bed, either. After yesterday's picnic supper and fishing, she wasn't looking forward to seeing either Paul or Bishop John. They'd acted like a couple of *kinner* the whole time, causing Barbara to wonder if they both might be vying for her attention.

Barbara swung her legs over the edge of the bed and rubbed her temples. She knew the bishop wanted to marry her, if only to help raise his girls. But why would Paul be trying to gain her attention? *He'll be going back to Pennsylvania soon and surely has no interest in me.* So why had he seemed so irritated by the bishop?

She stood and padded across the room to check on the baby. *Maybe I'm imagining things.* She stared down at her son, sleeping peacefully on his back, and thought about the baby's father. "Oh, David, why'd you have to die and leave me with four boys to raise and a business to run on my own? I feel so vulnerable and confused about everything right now."

Barbara glanced around the room she had shared with her husband for nearly ten years. Everything looked the same—their double bed and matching dresser, made by David's *daed;* the cedar chest at the foot of the bed, given to Barbara by her parents when she turned sixteen; the beautiful quilt Mom had made as a wedding present.

Her gaze came to rest on the *Biewel* lying on top of the dresser. It had been David's Bible, and she always found a measure of comfort in simply holding it in her hands.

Barbara left the crib and made her way across the room. As she picked up the Bible, tears coursed down her cheeks. The feel of the leather cover made her think about the harness shop. Should she sell the business and hope to make enough money so they could live off it? She certainly couldn't rely on her folks to support her and the boys. It was all Dad could do to help part-time in the shop. But the wages she gave him were a much-needed supplement to the meager income he and Mom made selling some of their garden produce and the quilts Mom made. Dad's arthritis had kept him from farming for quite a spell, and even though Barbara's sisters often sent money to their folks, she still felt the need to assist her parents as much as she could.

"Of course, I could sell the shop to Paul and marry the bishop," she said with a weary sigh as she took a seat on the edge of her bed again. She opened the

Bible to a place marked with a slip of paper. In the book of James, David had underlined the fifth verse of chapter one. " 'If any of you lack wisdom, let him ask of God, that giveth to all men liberally, and upbraideth not, and it shall be given him,' " she read aloud.

Setting the Bible aside, Barbara closed her eyes. "I'm so confused, Lord. I need Your wisdom. I need to know what to do about the bishop's offer of marriage, the harness shop, and my feelings toward Paul."

She released a shuddering sigh and thought about the verse of scripture from Ecclesiastes John had quoted to her awhile back, about two being better than one. Maybe she did need someone to share her life with. But could she ever be truly happy married to the bishop?

Truth be told, Barbara was falling in love with Paul, not John, but she couldn't let him know that. If they were meant to be together, he'd have to make the first move and let her know he felt the same way.

Barbara stood. It was time to set her thoughts aside and turn them over to God. She needed to wake the boys up, start breakfast, and get ready for church. "I'm going to pray for wisdom and leave my future in God's hands, just as David always did." She shook her head. "And I'm not going to let a little old headache keep me from worshiping the Lord today."

Paul had a hard time keeping his thoughts on the service and not on Barbara, who sat directly across from him. She held the baby in her arms, wide awake but quiet. On one side of Barbara sat her mother, and the bishop's oldest daughter occupied the other spot. Paul wondered if it was merely a coincidence or if John Frey had asked Betty to sit beside the woman he hoped to marry.

It was all Paul could do to keep from staring at Barbara's dimpled cheeks, which were slightly pink, no doubt from the heat inside the Zooks' house, caused by this warm summer morning. He wished he were free to fall in love with her and stay here in Webster County. But there were too many complications to prevent them from having a relationship.

He thought about yesterday's trip to the pond. Despite his irritation over the bishop, he had enjoyed being with Barbara and her boys. With the exception of Aaron, who remained aloof, her children had really warmed up to him. Even the baby seemed content when Paul held him, and the little guy sure was soft and cuddly. When the infant nestled against Paul's chest, it made him feel loved and appreciated.

The bishop's booming voice drove Paul's thoughts to the back of his mind. "The Bible says, 'For the Lord God will help me; therefore shall I not be confounded: therefore have I set my face like a flint, and I know that I shall not be ashamed.' Isaiah 50:7."

John Frey was preaching on challenges, and Paul wondered if the verse of scripture he'd just quoted was an announcement of the man's personal challenge to win Barbara's hand in marriage.

At the moment, Bishop Frey's face looked like it

was set in flint. He pursed his lips and held the Bible in front of him as though it were a weapon.

Paul stared at the floor. *Maybe his message is directed at me. Could be he wants me to realize how determined he is to make Barbara his wife.*

It didn't seem likely the man would bring his personal life into the sermon he'd prepared. But the bishop was only human, not perfect.

Paul was pretty sure John had God on his side, him being a spiritual leader and all. Still, that shouldn't give him an edge with Barbara, at least not to Paul's way of thinking.

When the bishop closed with prayer, Paul breathed a sigh of relief. He needed to get outside for some fresh air.

Barbara was glad when church was over and lunch had been served. She left the baby with her mother-in-law and allowed the three boys to play with their friends. She wanted to speak with Faith and ask for prayer concerning her situation.

Barbara spotted her friend on the other side of the yard. She'd just started heading that way when she came across the bishop talking to his daughter Betty.

Not wishing to interrupt their conversation, Barbara started to turn away. But at that moment she heard Betty mention her name. Curious, she ducked behind a tree.

"I don't understand why you're chasin' after Barbara Zook, Papa," Betty said.

"I'm tryin' to find you and your sisters a mother," her father replied. "Barbara would make a *gut mamm,* don't ya think?"

"Maybe so, but as far as I can tell; we've been gettin' along fine since Mama died."

"You might believe that to be so, but the truth is, things aren't done around the house the same as your *mamm* used to do."

Barbara drew in a deep breath and held it a few seconds. What made John Frey think his daughter would do things the way his wife had? Didn't the man realize every woman had her own ways?

"Besides," Betty went on to say, "addin' four boys to the family would be a handful."

"I rather like the idea of havin' a couple of boys around," he said with the voice of conviction. "Sure would be nice to have a few sets of strong hands in a couple years to do some of the harder chores. I could use some help with the bulk seed and garden supplies."

Betty cleared her throat. "Papa . . ."

"Yes, Betty?"

"Do you love Barbara?"

Barbara pushed her body against the tree and waited breathlessly for the bishop's reply.

"Well, I—" he sputtered.

"You don't, do you?"

"There's a lot more involved in marriage than a bunch of romantic nonsense. Besides, I need a woman companion. And love can be learned."

"Did you love Mama?"

"Of course I did. Loved her from the first moment I laid eyes on her."

There was a brief pause before Betty spoke again. "Papa, I hope you do remarry someday. But it needs to be for love, not convenience, or even to have a *mamm* for me and my sisters."

He grunted. "Guess I'll have to think on that awhile."

"Glad to hear it."

Barbara felt relief hearing it, as well. Maybe after his talk with Betty, Bishop John wouldn't be so anxious to pursue Barbara or expect an answer to his proposal of marriage anytime soon. She needed more time to think and pray about the situation.

When she felt the coast was clear, Barbara stepped out from behind the tree. She saw the bishop walking toward the barn and Betty heading to the house. Faith was still on the other side of the yard, talking with a group of women. Barbara would seek her out and visit awhile, then see how Mavis was managing with the baby.

A short while later, Barbara and Faith were seated on the grass under the shade of a hickory tree.

"You're lookin' a bit down in the mouth today," Faith said. "Are you still feelin' *hundsiwwel?*"

Barbara shrugged. "Oh, I'm done with the post-partum depression."

"Then why the long face?"

"I'm struggling with several issues," Barbara admitted. "Things I really need to talk about, if you're willing to listen."

138

Faith nodded, her blue eyes revealing obvious interest. "What issues are you strugglin' with?"

"The bishop and Paul."

Faith tipped her head in question.

"John wants me to marry him."

"I suspected as much."

"He's been over to my house a couple of times, askin' me to go places with him, but I've always turned him down."

"So he knows you're not interested?"

Barbara shook her head. "He was at the pond yesterday when Paul and I arrived with the boys."

Faith's mouth dropped open. "You went there with Paul again?"

"Jah."

Faith tapped her fingers along the side of her head. "I should have guessed what was goin' on."

"What's that supposed to mean?"

"I can see by the look on your face that you're smitten with the man."

Barbara wanted to deny it, but Faith knew her too well. "Paul and I don't see eye to eye on some things concerning the harness shop," she said. "But for some reason I'm attracted to him, though I can't figure out why."

Faith leaned her head back and laughed.

"What's so funny?"

"Don't try to figure out love, my friend. When two people fall for each other, they can be as different as sandpaper and polished cotton, yet still the feelin's are there, and you can't do a thing to stop 'em."

Barbara moaned. "I don't know how Paul feels about me."

"He's invited you to go fishin' with him twice. I'd say that says somethin' about his interest."

Barbara frowned. "At times he seems as if he cares, but there are other times when he's rather distant."

Faith clicked her tongue. "Ever since Adam met Eve, there has been trouble between men and women. Just 'cause Paul doesn't always see things the same as you, that doesn't mean he's not interested."

Barbara was about to comment when a ruckus on the lawn interrupted their conversation. She turned to see what was going on and was taken by surprise when she saw Joseph hollering and running after Faith's son, Isaiah, with a squirt gun.

"Now, where in the world did he get that?" Barbara muttered as she scrambled to her feet.

"Guess we'd better put our conversation on hold and see about our boys before one of 'em ends up crying." Faith shook her head. "Most likely it'll be Isaiah, unless his big sister comes to the rescue."

Barbara marched across the yard, planted herself in front of Joseph, and reached for the squirt gun.

Swish! A spurt of water hit her right in the face.

"Give me that!" she ordered. "What's gotten into you? And where did you get this squirt gun?"

Joseph's brows furrowed, and he pointed across the yard. "Paul Hilty gave it to me."

sixteen

Barbara hurried across the lawn to where Paul stood talking to Faith's husband. "Excuse me, Noah," she said, "but I need to speak with Paul a few minutes."

"No problem." He smiled and moved off in the direction of his wife, who stood near the boys.

"What's up?" Paul asked with raised eyebrows.

"Would you mind tellin' me why you gave my son a squirt gun to play with?" she asked, handing him the item in question.

He shoved the toy inside his shirt pocket and looked at her as though she were daft. "Didn't see any harm in it. The boy said he was hot, so I figured this would get him cooled off some."

"But he was squirtin' other *kinner*." She wrinkled her nose. "Besides, I don't cotton to the idea of my boys pointin' a gun at anyone—not even a toy one."

Paul's ears turned bright red. "Sorry," he mumbled. "I didn't think there'd be any problem." He shrugged. "At least this time you're not chewing me out for anything related to the harness shop."

His statement caught Barbara off guard. Was she always chewing him out? Did Paul think all she ever did was nag? If that were so, then he obviously had no romantic interest in her.

Unable to look him in the eye, she lowered her gaze. "I—I'm sorry for snappin'. It's just that I would have preferred it if you'd checked with me first about the

141

squirt gun. Then I could have explained my reasons."

"You're right. I shouldn't have given Joseph the toy without asking you." He touched her chin with his fingertips and raised it so they were looking at each other.

Shivers shimmied up Barbara's spine as Paul leaned closer and stared intently at her. If she hadn't known better, she might have believed he was about to kiss her. But that was ridiculous. There were others milling about who would notice if he did such a bold thing. Besides, *why* would Paul want to kiss someone who'd chewed him out the way she'd just done?

"You're kind of cute when you're mad, you know that?" he whispered, making little circles on Barbara's chin with his thumb.

She swallowed hard, unable to pull away from his gaze until she felt a tug on her apron.

Barbara glanced down. Aaron stood staring up at her with a questioning expression.

"Did you need me for somethin', son?"

He nodded. "Is it all right if I spend the night at Gabe Schwartz's? He and his family hired a driver to take 'em to Springfield tomorrow mornin'. They're gonna see Bass Pro Shops and do some other fun stuff."

"I don't know, Aaron," she said. "Paul might be needin' you in the harness shop tomorrow."

Paul shook his head. "Your *daed* said he's free in the morning, and his arthritic fingers are feeling better. So

I think we can manage okay without Aaron, don't you?"

Barbara deliberated a few seconds. Her oldest child had been moody and sad ever since David died. This was the first spark of the old Aaron she'd seen in a long time. Maybe she should let the boy have a good time with his friend.

Finally, she nodded. "*Jah,* okay. You can go."

Aaron clasped her hand. "*Danki.* I'll ask Gabe's *daed* to stop by our house on their way home today so I can get a change of clothes."

Barbara smiled at his enthusiasm. "Don't forget your toothbrush and comb. Wouldn't want my boy goin' off to the big city lookin' like a ragamuffin."

Aaron snickered, and she gave him a hug. "You be good now, ya hear?"

"I will, Mama." The child scampered off toward Gabe, who stood waiting across the yard.

"Seemed real eager, didn't he?" Paul asked.

Barbara nodded. "Aaron and Gabe have been *gut* friends since they were little fellows."

"Sure wish he'd see me in a more friendly light," Paul said in a wistful tone.

Barbara sighed. "Give him time, Paul." As the words slipped out, she wondered *why* she'd bothered to say them. She would be back working full time soon, and she was sure it would only be a matter of days before Paul would announce his intention to go back to Pennsylvania. If only she hadn't allowed herself to fall in love with the man.

• • •

On Monday morning, as Barbara headed to the harness shop, she decided to inform Paul that she could manage on her own now. If she gave him the option of leaving, and he took it, she'd know he had no interest in developing a relationship with her.

As she drew closer to the shop, she noticed that Paul's buggy wasn't parked outside. *Strange,* she thought as she opened the front door. *He's always here early—usually before Dad or me.*

Barbara spotted her father working at the riveting machine. He smiled and nodded in her direction. "*Gude mariye,* daughter."

"Mornin', Dad. I'm surprised to see you pressing rivets. It's not like Paul to be late to work."

Dad stepped away from the machine and placed the piece of leather he was holding on the wooden table nearby. "He dropped by a little bit ago. Wanted me to let you know he wouldn't be in today."

She wrinkled her forehead. "He's not sick, I hope."

"*Nee.* His *daed* fell off a ladder in their barn this momin'. An ambulance had to be called to take him to the hospital in Springfield."

Barbara's breath caught in her throat. "That's terrible! How bad was he hurt, do you know?"

He shook his head. "Paul didn't have any information yet. He hired a driver to take him to the hospital straightaway. Said he'd let us know as soon as he could what the doctors had to say about his *daed's* condition."

"I sure hope it's nothing serious. We've had enough tragedy in our community lately."

"You're right about that." Barbara's father patted her shoulder. "We need to pray."

Paul paced the length of the hospital waiting room, anxious for some report on Pop's condition. Doctors had been running tests on him for the last couple of hours, and Paul worried that might mean something was seriously wrong.

"Won't you please stop that pacin'?" his mother said from the bench where she sat across the room. She blinked her dark eyes and tucked a wayward strand of grayish-brown hair back into her bun.

He came to a halt in front of the window and stared out at the cloudy sky. It looked like they might get rain soon, which seemed fitting for an already gloomy Monday morning.

"I wonder why Monroe and Elam aren't back yet," Mom said, pulling Paul from his musings. "Shouldn't take them this long to get a few cups of coffee. I sure could use some about now."

Paul clenched and unclenched his fingers. How could Mom be worried about coffee when her husband was in the emergency room and they didn't know how badly he'd been hurt? *Maybe it's just Mom's way of trying to take her mind off the situation,* he decided. *I know how much she loves Pop.*

"Maybe you should head down the hall and see what's takin' them so long," she said.

Paul turned to face his mother. "I'm sure my brothers will be back in due time. They don't need me to go traipsing after them."

Mom grabbed a magazine from the table in front of her. "Sorry. I just figured it would give you somethin' to do besides wear the soles of your boots down as you walk back and forth across the waitin' room."

Paul was about to comment when a middle-aged nurse stepped into the room. "Joann Hilty?" she said, looking at Paul's mother.

Mom nodded and stood.

"Your husband is done with his tests. He's been moved to a private room now, so if you wish to see him, please follow me."

Mom's face was pinched, and deep lines etched her forehead. "Is Moses gonna be all right? What did the tests reveal?"

The nurse offered a weak smile. "The doctor will fill you in on all the details."

Paul started to follow his mother, but she stopped him. "You'd better wait here for your brothers; else they won't know where we are and might get worried."

Paul looked at the nurse. "What room is my dad in?"

"Second floor, room 202."

"Okay." Paul nodded. "Me, Monroe, and Elam will be there as soon as they get back."

seventeen

Barbara had just closed up shop for the day when Paul Hilty pulled into the yard. Anxious for news on his father, she hurried to his buggy and waited for him to climb down.

"How's your *daed?*" she asked when he stood beside her on the grass.

"He broke a couple ribs, bruised his left elbow real good, and pulled a muscle in his back." Paul shook his head. "He'll live, but he'll be in traction for the next few days."

Barbara breathed a sigh of relief. At least Moses Hilty's wounds would heal, and they wouldn't have to face another death in the community right now. "I'm sorry about your *daed's* accident, but I'm glad it wasn't any worse."

"Me, too."

"Guess he'll be laid up awhile, huh?"

Paul nodded soberly. "Pop won't be farming for several weeks." He shifted his weight in an uneasy manner. "I . . . uh . . . was wondering if you'd be able to get by without my help at the harness shop. I promised Pop I'd help Monroe and Elam in the fields until he's back on his feet."

Barbara's heart started to hammer. She knew the day would come when Paul would stop working in her shop, and she thought she'd prepared herself for it. But now she wasn't sure she could bear to hear the words.

He shook his head. "Things haven't been good between my *daed* and me for some time. I want to show him I care by helping him in this time of need."

"I understand." Barbara nibbled on the inside of her cheek. "I'm feelin' stronger now, so I think Dad and I can manage fine on our own."

She wondered if she should tell Paul he was free to return to Lancaster County after his *daed* healed up. *Better not say anything just now,* she decided. *It can be said later, when Paul's done helping his brothers.*

Paul shuffled his boots and stared at the ground. "Well, guess I'd better be going."

Barbara noticed his forlorn expression. Probably worried about his *daed* and not really looking forward to working the fields.

Impulsively, she reached out and touched his arm. "How'd you like to join me and the family for supper tonight? We're plannin' to eat outside at the picnic table with Mom and Dad."

Paul hesitated, but only for a moment. Then his lips curved into a wide smile. "Sounds real *gut*. I'd be much obliged."

Barbara nodded toward the house. "Come along, then. You can relax on the porch swing with a cold drink while I go next door to my folks' place and get the *kinner.*"

Paul leaned against the quilted pillows propped on the back of the porch swing, sipping the lemonade Barbara had given him before she went next door. It sure felt nice to sit a spell and enjoy the cool evening breeze. He drew in a deep breath and savored the aroma of country air. Soon fall would be here, and then there'd be crisp fallen leaves and bonfires to enjoy. He'd always liked autumn, especially here, where life was more easygoing than back in Lancaster County.

Paul dosed his eyes and let his imagination run wild. In his mind's eye, he saw Barbara sitting in the wicker rocking chair on her front porch. In her lap was a baby, but it wasn't Davey. The *boppli* he envisioned was a dark-eyed little girl with shiny blond hair.

Instinctively, he reached up and touched the side of his head. *Hair just like mine,* he mused. *What would my life be like if I could stay right here, marry Barbara, and have a few* kinner *of my own?* Was it a foolish dream, or could Barbara possibly open her heart and home to him? With each passing day, he'd fallen harder for her, which wasn't a good thing if she didn't have the same feelings toward him.

"You sleepin', Paul?"

Paul jerked upright and snapped his eyes open. He'd had no idea Joseph was standing there, and he wondered how long the boy had been watching him.

"I was restin' my eyes, son," he said with a smile. "It's been a long day."

Joseph's forehead wrinkled. "I heard Mama tell Grandma you've been at the hospital with your *daed.*"

"That's right. He fell off a ladder in the barn this morning and banged himself up pretty good."

"Sorry to hear that. I'll say a prayer for him."

"That'd be nice. I'm sure he'd appreciate all the prayers he can get."

Joseph's eyes brightened. "Mama also said you'd be joinin' us for supper tonight. I'm right glad about that."

"Me, too." Paul patted the empty spot on the swing beside him. "Want to join me awhile?"

The boy scrambled onto the swing and cuddled against Paul's side.

"You miss your *daed?*" Paul asked.

"*Jah.*"

"That's understandable. I'm sure your *mamm* and brothers miss him, too."

"I know Mama does. She cries when she's alone in her room sometimes. I think it's 'cause she's pinin' for Papa."

Paul's heart clenched. *It's a shame for such a young boy to lose his father. Doesn't seem right. But then many things happen in life that aren't fair.*

They sat in silence awhile, Paul pumping the swing back and forth and Joseph humming softly.

"Sure wish you were my *daed* now," the boy blurted out.

"Don't know if that's possible," Paul said, giving the child's hand a gentle squeeze. "But I hope I'll always be your friend."

Joseph leaned away and stared up at Paul. His dark eyes were wide and his face ever so solemn. "Aaron says Bishop John is after Mama to marry him."

"And what do you think about that?"

Joseph shook his head. "Don't like it. Not one little bit." He pushed his weight against Paul again. "It's you I want, nobody else."

A lump formed in Paul's throat. In all his grown-up years, he'd never had a kid take to him the way Joseph had. It made him long to be a father—Joseph's father, anyway.

"Can you marry my *mamm* and be my *dad?*"

Paul patted the boy's knee. "It's not that simple, son."

"Seems simple enough to me. You just go right up to her and ask. That wouldn't be so hard, would it?"

The back door of the Rabers' house opened and Barbara stepped out, carrying the baby, with Zachary and Aaron at her side. Paul was glad for the interruption. At least he didn't have to come up with an answer for Joseph's question. It was a question that had been rolling around in his own head for the past couple of days.

Paul stood and followed Barbara and the boys into her house. Once inside the kitchen, Barbara placed little David in his baby carriage, instructing Zachary to push it back and forth if the infant got fussy. Aaron and Joseph were asked to haul pitchers of lemonade and iced tea out to the picnic table, while Barbara busied herself at the cupboard, slicing thick hunks of juicy-looking ham.

Paul's stomach rumbled. He'd spent most of the day at the hospital and hadn't taken the time for anything other than a few cups of coffee and a stale doughnut his brothers had brought from the cafeteria. Since Mom had decided to stay at her husband's side awhile longer, Paul figured he'd have to manage on his own for supper. Barbara's invitation had been a pleasant surprise, for more than one reason. Not only would his hunger be satisfied, but he was being offered an opportunity to spend time with Barbara again, even if they would have her parents and the boys as chaperones.

"Anything I can do to help?" he asked. "I'm sure you're tired after a long day at the shop."

She shook her head but kept her back to him. "Dad and I managed okay, and I'm not feelin' too done in."

"Even so, I'd like to do more than stand here by the wall and watch."

"If you really want to do somethin', you can check the *boppli*'s *wendels*."

Paul's eyebrows shot up. Did she really expect him to change a diaper?

"Just kidding," she said with a muffled snicker. "Mom made sure Davey's diaper was clean and dry before I showed up to get the boys."

"She's been a big help to you since David died, huh?"

"*Jah.* Don't know what I'd have done without her or Dad." She turned to face him. "I don't want to be dependent on their help forever, though. Sooner or later I'll have to make it on my own."

For want of anything better to do, Paul pulled out a chair and took a seat at the table. "Guess you could always take the bishop up on his offer of marriage."

Barbara dropped the knife to the cupboard with a clatter and spun around. "You really think I should?"

He wanted to tell her right then that it was him she should marry. But she'd never given any indication that she cared for him that way, and unless she did . . . He shrugged. "It's none of my business."

Barbara studied him a few seconds, as if she were waiting for him to say more. Was she hoping he'd tell her not to marry the bishop? Did his opinion even matter?

She reached for her knife again and started cutting the meat.

"Are you considering it, then?" Paul had to know. If she were the least bit interested in the bishop, he would back off, plain and simple.

"Told him I'd think on it, that's all," she replied.

Paul leaned both elbows on the table. "And have you?"

"Jah."

"He's some older than you, ain't it so?"

"That's true enough."

"And being married to a bishop would put an extra burden on you."

"Probably."

"What of the harness shop?"

"What about it?"

"Would you sell the place if you were to marry John?"

"Guess I'd have to, seein' as how I'd be takin' on the

responsibility of helpin' raise his four daughters, plus my boys."

Paul grabbed a napkin from the basket in the center of the table and wadded it into a tight ball. The thought of Barbara marrying the bishop was enough to make him lose his appetite. Still, he couldn't seem to muster the courage to speak on his own behalf.

"I thought you loved running the harness shop," he said. "How could you give up something you enjoy doing so much?"

Barbara shrugged her slim shoulders. "One does what one has to do in a time of need." She sliced the last piece of ham and placed it on the platter. "But I haven't decided yet."

eighteen

Paul couldn't believe he'd been helping his brothers a whole week already. Every day, he trudged back to his folks' house at the end of the day, sweat-soaked and dirty from head to toe, while Monroe and Elam went home to their families.

Pop had been released from the hospital three days ago, but due to the pain in his ribs and back, he was pretty much confined to bed. He was also cranky as a mule with a tick in its backside.

Due to his dad's condition, Paul tried hard to be kind and patient. However, his patience had been tested yesterday when Pop summoned him to his room and proceeded to tell Paul that if his back didn't heal up right, he might never be able to work in the fields again—at least not for any length of time. That being the case, Monroe and Elam would need another pair of hands on a regular basis—namely, Paul's hands.

Seeing how much pain his *daed* was in, Paul had merely said he would think on it. But today he was prepared to state his case before he lost his nerve.

When Paul entered the kitchen, Mom turned from her place at the stove and clicked her tongue. "You surely do look a mess, son. Hardly a speck of skin showin' that's not covered with dust."

He nodded. "I'm heading upstairs to wash. Then I need to speak to Pop before supper."

"Take your time," she replied. "The meal won't be ready for another thirty minutes or so."

Paul left the room. After he'd cleaned off most of the field dirt, he went into his parents' room. Pop was sitting up in bed, leaning against a stack of pillows, reading from the Bible.

"How you feeling today?"

"How'd it go in the fields?"

They'd both spoken at the same time. As Paul stepped to the side of the bed, he said, "You go first, Pop."

His dad set the Bible aside and motioned to a nearby chair. "Have a seat and tell me how your work's goin'."

Paul did as his father suggested. "It's coming along okay. We should be ready to harvest the hay and corn in a few more weeks." Paul clasped his hands tightly together. "I . . . uh . . . how's your back?"

"Feels fine as long as I don't move." Pop grimaced. "I'm supposed to be startin' physical therapy tomorrow mornin'. Sure don't relish that."

"It should help your muscles relax."

"*Jah,* well, I don't much like the idea of anyone pushin' and shovin' on my spine." Pop shifted on the pillow and groaned. "I have to wonder if I'll ever get back to workin' in the fields."

Paul felt as if a heavy weight rested on his chest. The thought of giving up work in the harness shop to help with the farming made Paul's heart ache.

He leaned forward, resting his elbows on his knees. "I've been thinking on the things we talked about yesterday."

Pop turned his head and looked directly at Paul. *"Jah?"*

Paul swallowed around the nodule lodged in his throat. He hated to upset Pop when he was hurting, but the things on his mind couldn't wait forever. No use getting his *daed's* hopes up.

"I know you're not able to work right now, and I said I'd help in the fields 'til you're better, but—"

"Are you backin' out of our agreement?" Pop narrowed his eyes.

Paul shook his head. "*Nee.* I'll help Monroe and Elam until we get caught up and the harvesting is done. But after that I'll be returning to Pennsylvania." He gave his left earlobe a couple of pulls. "Been gone a lot longer than I'd planned already."

"What about Barbara Zook?"

"What about her?"

"I thought you were needed to help in her harness shop."

"I was. But her *daed's* doing better, and she's back at work full time, so she doesn't really need me anymore." *But I'd stay if she asked me to,* Paul thought. *I'd proclaim my love for her and stay on as her husband if there was any indication she loved me and would agree to become my wife.*

Pop blew out his breath. "So you're sayin' you'll hang around 'til the harvest is done; then you plan to head back to Pennsylvania?"

"*Jah,* that's right."

"And nothin' I can say will change your mind?"

Paul shook his head. "Sorry. I enjoy working with leather and never have cottoned to farmwork."

"How well I know that," Pop agreed with a nod. "Even when you was a boy, you complained about all the dust and long hours in the fields."

"You understand the way I feel, then?"

"I recognize your desire to do what makes you happy. If it becomes necessary, I'll hire someone to help your brothers in the fields."

Paul reached out and touched his father's hand. The change in Pop's attitude was like a miracle. An answer to prayer, that's what it was. *"Danki,"* he murmured. "I appreciate that."

"You'll be missed when you leave Webster County," Pop added.

Paul nodded. "I'll miss you all, too."

• • •

Barbara stared out the shop window, watching Aaron and Joseph hike up the driveway that led to the road where the one-room schoolhouse was located. Today was the first day after summer break, and Joseph's first time to attend school.

"You worried about the boys?" Dad asked as he stepped up behind her.

She turned to face him. "Just Joseph. He's so young yet. I hope he does okay and doesn't give Ruth Yoder a hard time." She sighed. "I wish my sister still taught school here. He might feel more secure having his aunt Sarah as his teacher."

"I hear tell Ruth's done a fine job of taking over for Sarah. I'm sure Joseph will do all right." Dad chuckled. "I remember when I attended school for the first time. Hated first grade and didn't care much for my teacher, but I sure did enjoy playin' on the teeter-totter out behind the schoolhouse during recess."

Barbara smiled. Dad was probably right. Joseph would do okay. He was an easygoing, obedient child and should get along fine with the teacher and his schoolmates. Aaron, on the other hand, was a bit contrite and could be a handful at times.

He's stubborn, just like his father, she mused. *But I'm sure he'll manage okay on this first day of school. Leastways, I pray 'tis so.*

"Sure seems different around here without Paul Hilty, don't ya think?"

Barbara acknowledged her father's question with a

158

brief nod. She hated to admit it, but she did miss Paul coming to work every day. Missed his friendly banter, sparkling blue eyes, and that lopsided grin. He'd been a big help and knew a lot about running a harness shop, even if they didn't see eye to eye on everything.

She knew Paul must be working hard at his father's farm. She'd thought about inviting him to join them for supper one night after work. But she'd set that idea aside, fearful he might get the impression she was interested in him. She was, of course, but didn't want him knowing that, since he hadn't revealed any feelings for her other than friendship.

And then there's Aaron, she thought as she turned away from the window. *He finally seems to be adjusting to his* daed's *death. But if Paul starts coming around when it's got nothing to do with work, Aaron might become upset again.*

Barbara wasn't sure why, but Aaron seemed to consider Paul a threat. The other children liked the man just fine. In Joseph's case, maybe a little too much. On the last Sunday they'd had church, the boy had hung around Paul all afternoon. She'd noticed him clinging to Paul's hand and really enjoying the piggyback rides Paul had graciously given to both Joseph and Zachary.

Paul will make a good daed *someday. But I'm afraid it's not going to be my boys he'll be fathering.*

Barbara grabbed a hunk of leather and dropped it into the washtub filled with dye. "Guess it's time to get somethin' constructive done."

"Yep," Dad agreed. "Sure won't happen on its

own, no matter how much I might wish it could."

Barbara's conscience pricked her heart. She knew the harness business wasn't Dad's true calling. Fact was, he'd much rather be tending his garden or relaxing on the porch than helping her keep the place running. But with Paul gone off to help his brothers, Barbara knew she couldn't make it on her own without Dad's help. So she took one day at a time, thanking the Lord for each hour that Dad felt well enough to lend a hand. She tried not to think about how it would be when the day finally came that he could no longer hold a piece of leather in his hands. How would she manage then? She'd have Aaron's help during his breaks from school, but to be on her own in the shop all the time would be nearly impossible.

Maybe I do need to give the bishop's offer of marriage more thought. I'd better pray harder about all of this.

Paul hadn't been back to Zook's Harness Shop since he told Barbara he'd be quitting to help his brothers on the farm. Today, he had no choice but to go there. One of the mules had busted its bridle in the field this afternoon, and it needed to be repaired right away.

There was a part of Paul that dreaded seeing Barbara again. Being around her evoked emotions he'd rather not deal with. But another part of him looked forward to seeing her beautiful face, her dark hair and eyes— eyes he could drown in—eyes that made him want to shout to the world that Barbara Zook had captured his heart.

Paul took the time to clean up after work before heading over to Barbara's place. He didn't want her to see him looking like a mess. As he pulled into the Zooks' driveway, he cringed when he saw John Frey standing beside his buggy outside of her shop.

"Doesn't that man ever give up?" he muttered.

Paul pulled his buggy alongside the bishop's and climbed down. "Afternoon, Bishop," he said, hoping his voice sounded more relaxed than he felt. "You here on business?"

John gave his beard a couple of tugs and squinted his beady eyes. "Was, but the business has been concluded. I'm on my way home now."

Good. I wasn't looking forward to watching you flirt with Barbara. Paul started for the front door of the harness shop. "See you around, then," he called over his shoulder.

"*Jah,* on Sunday if not before."

Paul turned the doorknob and stepped inside. He didn't see anyone at first and wondered if Barbara might have gone up to her folks' house to check on the boys. Even if she had, her *daed* should be here. The shop was still open for the day.

Paul cupped his hands around his mouth. "Anyone here?"

"Be right with you."

He shivered at the sound of Barbara's voice coming from the back room. He'd really missed her, and no

161

matter how much he tried to fight the feelings, Paul didn't think he would ever meet another woman who made him feel the way Barbara did.

A few minutes later, she headed his way, carrying a chunk of leather that looked much too weighty for her to be lugging.

Paul stepped forward and held out his hands. "Here, let me help you with that."

She hesitated a moment but finally turned the bundle over to him. *Danki*."

Paul placed the leather on the closest workbench. "This okay?"

She nodded. "What brings you by this afternoon? I figured you'd be hard at work in the fields yet."

He pointed to the broken bridle draped over his shoulder. "Had a little accident with the mules. This snapped right in two."

"I can try to get it fixed first thing in the mornin'," she said. "Will that be soon enough?"

"We really need to have it when we start work tomorrow. I was hoping you wouldn't mind if I did the repairs myself."

Her eyebrows lifted. "You mean now?"

"*Jah*. If it's okay with you." He paused and licked his lips, which seemed awfully dry all of a sudden. "I'll pay for any of the supplies I use, of course."

Barbara waved her hand. "Nonsense. Just help yourself to whatever you're needin'. It's the least I can do to say thanks for helpin' me out in my time of need."

He leaned slightly toward her. "Speaking of which

162

. . . how are you managing now? Is your *daed* able to be here all the time?"

She shrugged and released a little sigh. "He comes in every day but doesn't always work the whole time. His hands are botherin' him again, but he keeps at it the best he's able."

Paul's heart clenched, and he felt like he was being ripped in two. Pop needed him to work the fields, but it was obvious Barbara could still use his help here. Then there was his cousin Abe, who'd written and said he was getting really busy and wondered when Paul planned to return to Pennsylvania. Abe said he might have to hire another man if Paul didn't come back soon. Paul wasn't sure where he belonged anymore, or who needed him the most. The only thing he knew for certain was that he loved Barbara Zook. The question was, what, if anything, should he do about it?

nineteen

"Would you like to join us for supper?" Barbara asked as Paul was about to get into his buggy. "It'll just be me and the boys," she added with a look of uncertainty. "Mom and Dad are going into town to eat."

"I'd be happy to," Paul said with enthusiasm. This was the opportunity he'd been waiting for. With any luck, after her sons were finished eating, he'd have some time to be alone with Barbara, to tell her how he'd come to care for her, and hopefully to discover

163

how she felt about him. He didn't want to leave Webster County until he knew. Maybe, if his prayers were answered, he wouldn't have to leave at all.

He smiled to himself. *She must care a little, or she wouldn't have invited me to stay for supper.*

At Barbara's suggestion, Paul waited on the back porch while she went next door to get her brood. He took a seat on the top step and stared into the yard, overgrown with weeds again and direly in need of a good mowing.

Lord, give me the courage to open my heart to Barbara tonight. And if it's Your will for us to be together, help her to be receptive.

When he heard a door open and shut, Paul glanced at the Rabers's place. Joseph was the first to exit his grandparents' house, and he came bounding across the lawn like an excited puppy. As soon as he reached his own back porch, the child threw himself into Paul's arms.

"Mama said you're here for supper again."

"That's right." Paul ruffled the boy's blond hair.

"I'm ever so glad." Joseph nestled against Paul's chest, and once more, Paul was filled with a strong desire to marry and raise a family. Never had he felt so much love.

Barbara showed up then with Aaron, Zachary, and the baby. "Let's go inside, shall we?" she said with a smile that warmed Paul's heart.

"Sounds *gut* to me." Paul stood, and Joseph latched onto his hand.

"How was school today, Aaron?" Paul asked as the boy tromped up the steps behind his mother.

"Okay."

"Have you been helping your *mamm* in the harness shop after school and on Saturdays?"

"Sometimes."

Paul blew out his breath. So much for trying to make small talk with Barbara's oldest. It was apparent the boy wasn't near as happy to have Paul staying for supper as his younger brother seemed to be.

As soon as they entered the house, Aaron took off upstairs. Joseph pulled Paul into the kitchen and pointed to the rocking chair. "Why don't ya set a spell, and I'll sit with you?"

Paul looked at Barbara. When she nodded, he took a seat. Without invitation, Joseph crawled into his lap, and Zachary did the same. Paul couldn't help but wonder how it would feel to come home every day after work and be surrounded by his boys.

He began to rock, hoping the action would get him thinking straight again. These were Barbara's boys, not his. He had no right to be thinking such thoughts.

Barbara placed the sleeping baby in his carriage on the other side of the room and donned her choring apron. "Would soup and sandwiches be okay? I've got some leftover bean soup in the refrigerator." When she glanced at Paul, he noticed how tired she looked. Dark circles hung beneath her eyes, her cheeks were flushed, and her shoulders drooped with obvious fatigue.

"How can I help?" he asked. "Want me to set the table or make the sandwiches?"

Barbara presented Paul with a smile that let him know she was grateful for the offer. "The boys can set the table. If you've a mind to make the sandwiches, there's some barbecued beef in the refrigerator. Maybe you could get the soup out for me, too."

"Sure, no problem."

She looked at Joseph. "Take Zachary upstairs and see that you both get washed up. Tell Aaron to do the same. When you're done, I'd like all three of you to come back down and set the table."

Joseph leaned heavily against Paul's chest. "Promise you won't leave?"

Paul tweaked the boy's nose. " 'Course not."

The children climbed down and scampered out of the room. A few seconds later, Paul heard their footsteps clomping up the stairs.

Paul stood and headed for the refrigerator, where he retrieved a platter of shredded beef and the pot of bean soup. After Barbara lit the gas on the stove, Paul set the pot on the burner.

He grabbed the sandwich rolls off the cupboard and began to fill several with barbecued beef. He licked his lips as the tantalizing aroma of bean soup permeated the kitchen. His stomach rumbled, reminding him how hungry he was.

Should I say something to Barbara now about the way I feel? In spite of the sense of urgency that pulled on his heart, he decided he'd better wait until the boys were finished eating so he could speak to her without interruption.

All during supper Barbara had the feeling Paul wanted to say something to her—something important. He seemed kind of edgy, toying with his napkin and staring at her in an odd sort of way.

Does he care about me? Should I have allowed myself to have feelings for him, in spite of Aaron's attitude?

Determined to set her thoughts aside, Barbara finished her last bite of soup and pushed her chair away from the table.

Paul did the same, placing his empty bowl, plate, and spoon into the sink. "Barbara, I'd like to speak to you alone, if it's all right. Maybe we could sit outside on the porch?"

"That sounds nice. But I need to do up the dishes first."

"Why not let Aaron and Joseph do them? They're old enough, don't you think?" He turned to face the boys, who still sat at the table. "Maybe even little Zachary could help by clearing the rest of the table."

Joseph grinned as though he considered it a compliment that Paul thought him big enough to do the dishes. Aaron, however, glared at Paul, with a look of defiance glinting in his dark eyes.

"Ya got no right to be tellin' me or my brothers what to do," Aaron said boldly.

Paul stepped forward and turned his hands palms up. "It was only a suggestion to your *mamm.*"

Joseph grabbed his plate and scrambled out of his chair, hurrying toward the sink. "Boost me up, Mama, so I can do these dishes."

Barbara bent down and chucked her son under the chin. "If you're gonna be washin' dishes, you'll need a chair to stand on. I surely can't hold you the whole time."

Joseph turned to face Aaron. "Bring me a chair, would ya please?"

Aaron folded his arms in a stubborn, unyielding pose. "Get it yourself."

"What's gotten into you?" Barbara shook her finger. "Bring a chair over to the sink now, and apologize to your brother."

Aaron sat there looking straight ahead. Zachary kept eating his soup, too young to be aware of the tension in the room.

Barbara grimaced. She'd thought her oldest boy was doing better lately. She opened her mouth to reprimand Aaron, but Paul spoke first.

"Your mother's right. You do owe your brother an apology. And you owe your *mamm* one, too, for not doing as she told you to."

Aaron continued to sit there, unmoving.

Paul crossed the room, pulled out a chair beside the boy, and sat down. "What have you got to say for yourself?"

Aaron's shoulders slumped as he stared at the table.

Paul glanced at Barbara. He seemed to be asking for her permission to handle the situation.

"Go ahead, if you don't mind," she said, grabbing the closest chair and pushing it over to the sink. Joseph climbed onto the chair, and she helped him fill the dish tub with soap and water.

There was silence at the table, and Barbara wondered if she'd made a mistake letting Paul take charge of things. As soon as she was certain Joseph could handle the dishes on his own, she moved back to the table and took a seat across from Aaron.

"I don't know why you're actin' this way," she said sternly, "but I will not have you disobeyin' or spoutin' off like this, is that clear?"

The boy nodded soberly.

Paul reached over and touched Aaron's arm, but he jerked it away. Then Aaron turned his head and looked Paul squarely in the face. "You ain't my *daed*."

Paul opened his mouth, and so did Barbara. But before either could speak, Aaron pushed his chair aside, jumped up, and raced out the back door.

twenty

Paul stared out the kitchen window. "My *mamm* always said I ought to learn to keep my big mouth shut. Now I've made the boy mad."

"It's not your fault," Barbara said as she joined him at the window. "Aaron started acting moody and belligerent after David died. I thought he was getting better." She shrugged. "Guess I was wrong."

"Maybe I should go after him."

169

Barbara shook her head. "I think it's best if we let him be by himself awhile."

"But who's gonna help me with the dishes?" Joseph spoke up from his place at the sink.

Paul crossed the room and patted the boy's shoulder. "You wash and I'll dry. How's that sound?"

Joseph grinned up at him. "I'd like that." He looked over at Zachary, still sitting at the table dawdling with his bowl of soup. "Hurry up, ya slowpoke. We need them dishes."

"Let's get the ones in the sink done first," Paul suggested. "By then maybe your little brother will be finished."

"Okay."

If only my oldest son would be so compliant, Barbara thought. *Is it Aaron's personality, or have I failed him somehow?*

Just then the baby began to cry. Barbara turned her attention to the precious bundle lying in the carriage across the room.

"I need to feed and change Davey," she said to Paul. "If you'll excuse me, I'll be upstairs for a while."

He nodded as he took another clean dish from Joseph. At least, Barbara hoped the boy was getting them clean.

"Maybe by the time you come back to the kitchen, Aaron will have returned," Paul said in a reassuring tone.

Barbara felt his strength and kindness surround her like a warm quilt. For one wild moment, she had the crazy impulse to lean her head against his chest and feel the warmth of his embrace.

Pushing the ridiculous notion aside, she scooped the baby into her arms and started for the door leading to the upstairs. "Be back soon."

Paul glanced at the dock on the wall above the refrigerator. Barbara had been gone nearly an hour, and so had Aaron. He figured it was possible she might have fallen asleep while feeding the *boppli,* but why wasn't the boy back yet?

Paul had been keeping Zachary and Joseph entertained with an easy puzzle he'd found on a shelf in the kitchen. Now it was almost seven o'clock. He really should be getting home so he could do any final chores for the day.

Unsure of what to do, Paul opened the back door and stepped onto the porch. No sign of Aaron.

He stuck his head inside the kitchen doorway. "Joseph, I'm gonna run over to your grandma and grandpa's place a minute. Will you and Zachary be all right?"

The boy's head bobbed up and down. "Sure. We'll be fine. Mama's just upstairs, ya know."

"Okay. I'll be back quick as a wink." Paul bounded off the porch and raced over to the Rabers's house. He pounded on the door several times, but no one answered. Then he remembered that Barbara had said they'd gone out for supper. They probably weren't back yet.

Paul thought about looking for Aaron in the barn or harness shop, but he didn't want to leave Zachary and Joseph alone that long.

"I'd better get back inside," he muttered, turning toward Barbara's house. "No telling what those two little boys are up to."

When he entered the kitchen again, Paul discovered the children had helped themselves to cookies and milk. Joseph had a white mustache on his upper lip, and Zachary's face was dotted with chocolate. Cookie crumbs were strewn all over the table, and a puddle of milk lay under Zachary's chair.

Paul grabbed a dishrag from the kitchen sink and tossed it to Joseph. "You'd better get this mess cleaned up before your *mamm* comes downstairs."

While Joseph sopped up the milk, Zachary continued to nibble on his cookie.

Paul pulled a towel off the rack under the sink, dampened it with water, and sponged off the younger boy's face. He'd just finished when Barbara entered the kitchen.

"The *boppli*'s asleep in his crib, and—" She stopped short and stared at her sons.

"Looks like you've had yourselves a little party while I was gone."

"Me and Joseph eated cookies," Zachary announced, licking his fingers.

"So I see."

"They helped themselves when I went outside to see if Aaron had gone to your folks' place," Paul explained.

Barbara glanced around the room. "Aaron's not back yet?" Alarm showed clearly on her face.

Paul took the dishrag and towel back to the sink and turned to face her. "I thought about going out looking for Aaron, but I didn't want to leave the younger ones alone that long."

Barbara's gaze went to the window. "I'm worried."

"Tell me where his favorite places are, and I'll see if I can find him," Paul said. His chores could wait. Right now, finding the boy was more important.

Barbara rubbed her forehead. "Let's see . . . He likes to play in the barn." She continued to massage her head, making little circles with her fingertips. "He enjoys bein' in the harness shop, of course."

"I'll look around the yard real good, then go to the shop." Paul headed for the back door. "Try not to worry. I'm sure he's fine."

As Paul made his way across the yard, he thought about his plan to speak with Barbara about their relationship. It didn't look like he was going to get that chance. Not tonight, anyway.

Barbara had been pacing the kitchen floor for the last half hour. Where was Aaron, and why wasn't Paul back with a report? She was tempted to gather up the boys and go looking herself, but the baby was asleep, and the other two needed to be put to bed soon, as well.

She glanced out the window one more time. It was getting dark, and as far as she could tell, her folks still weren't back from town. She'd been watching for them, hoping Dad could join Paul in the search for Aaron.

Barbara closed her eyes and clasped her hands tightly together. *Please, Lord, let my boy be okay.*

"Mama, Zachary's hidin' pieces of puzzle on me," Joseph whined.

"Am not," Zachary retorted.

"Are so."

"Huh-uh."

"*Jah,* I seen you slip one onto your chair."

"Stop it!" Barbara's nerves felt like taut rubber bands. She forced herself to breathe deeply and count to ten. No good could come from yelling at the boys just because she was upset over Aaron's disappearance.

This is my fault, she thought miserably. *I should have sent Aaron to his room as soon as he started mouthing off. I'll never forgive myself if anything bad has happened to my oldest son.*

Paul closed the door of the harness shop and stepped onto the grass. Aaron wasn't in the shop, nor was he anywhere in the yard. Paul had checked every conceivable hiding spot outdoors. His next stop would be the barn. If Aaron wasn't there, he didn't know where else to look.

Maybe he wandered off the property and headed down the road to his friend Gabe's. If he's not in the barn, I'd better hitch my horse to the buggy and go there.

Paul entered the barn. It was dark and smelled of hay and animals. He cupped his hands around his mouth. "Aaron, you in here?"

The only response was a nicker from the buggy horses.

Paul located a gas lantern and struck a match. A circle of light encompassed the area where he stood. He held the lantern overhead and moved slowly about the building. "Aaron!" he called several times.

No answer.

As he continued to circle the barn, looking in every nook and cranny, Paul noticed the door to the silo was open. On a hunch, he stepped through the opening.

"Anybody here?" he hollered.

"Help!"

Paul cocked his head and listened.

"Help me, please!"

"Aaron, is that you?"

"*Jah*. I'm up here."

Paul held the light overhead and looked upward into the empty silo. His heart nearly stopped beating when he saw Aaron standing on the top rung of the ladder.

"What are you doing up there, boy? Don't you know how dangerous that is?"

"I–I climbed up to be by myself, but I got scared and couldn't get back down."

Paul gulped as a familiar feeling of terror swept over him. He hated high places. Had ever since he was a boy and had gotten himself stuck in a tree. He hadn't been able to talk any of his brothers into helping him down and had ended up falling and breaking his leg. Ever since then he'd been deathly afraid of heights.

"C—c—can ya help me get down?" Aaron pleaded.

With his heart hammering in his chest, Paul drew in a deep breath and hung the lantern on a nearby nail. "I'm coming, Aaron. Hang on."

twenty-one

Paul's hands turned sweaty and his legs trembled as he drew in a deep breath, grabbed hold of the ladder, and slowly ascended it. *Don't think about where you are. Don't look down. Take one rung at a time.*

Lord, ease my fears and help me do this.

"I'm really scared," Aaron cried from above. "My hands hurt from holdin' on so tight. I feel like I'm gonna fall."

A chill rippled through Paul. What if the child let go? "Be still, Aaron. I'm almost there." He didn't want to admit it, but Paul figured he was probably more afraid than the boy. *With God's help I'll get Aaron back into his mother's arms.*

When he reached the rung directly below Aaron, Paul wrapped his arms around the boy and held him tightly for a few seconds. Aaron stiffened at first but then relaxed. Paul did the same.

The child sniffed. "How are you gonna get me down?"

"We'll go the same way we came up—one rung at a

time." Paul released one hand from around Aaron's waist and grabbed hold of the rung where the boy stood.

"Don't let me go." Aaron's voice shook with emotion, and Paul's fears for himself abated. Aaron was his first priority, and all that mattered was getting Barbara's son safely to the ground.

"I'm gonna hold you around the middle with one hand, and we'll inch our way down the ladder together. Are you ready now?"

"I—I think so."

"Step with your left foot until you feel it touch the rung below. And whatever you do, don't look down."

Aaron did as he was told. Slowly, rung by rung, the two of them descended the ladder. All the while, Paul kept one arm around Aaron's waist and whispered comforting words in his ear. "We're gonna make it, son. Almost there; just a few more rungs."

When Paul's feet finally touched the ground, he lifted Aaron with both hands, turning the child to face him.

Aaron clung to him tearfully. "I ain't never goin' up there again."

Paul patted Aaron's back as the boy's tears dampened his shirt. "It's okay now. You're gonna be all right."

"I–I shouldn't have run off like I did. Shouldn't have climbed the silo ladder, either." Aaron hiccupped. "I'm sorry for spoutin' off back at the house."

"All's forgiven. It's behind us now."

When Aaron's tears subsided, Paul set him on the ground. "Know what?"

"What?"

"I've been afraid of heights ever since I was a boy. Climbing up that ladder had me scared half to death."

Aaron's dark eyes grew large. "Really?"

"Yep."

"Ya ain't just sayin' that to make me feel better?"

"Nope. It's the truth, plain and simple."

"Then why'd ya do it?"

"Because I care about you, son." The words came surprisingly easy, and Paul paused as he thought about what to say next. This was the chance he'd been waiting for with Aaron, and he didn't want to mess it up by saying the wrong thing. "I know I can never take your *daed*'s place, and I'm not trying to," he assured the boy. "All I want is for us to be friends."

Aaron's lower lip quivered. "It was brave of you to climb up and rescue me. I'll never forget it. *Danki*."

"You're welcome." Paul gave Aaron's shoulder a gentle squeeze. "I think we'd better head back to the house now, don't you?"

"I guess. But I'll probably be in big trouble for bein' gone so long and all."

"Your *mamm* has been worried about you."

"You think she'll be mad?"

Paul shrugged. "That's hard to say. When I was a boy and did something my *mamm* disapproved of, I always knew she loved me, even if I ended up getting a sound *bletching*."

Aaron's eyes were wide. "You think Mama's gonna give me the switch?"

"I doubt it. Seems to me she'll just be glad to see you're okay."

"Guess I'd better take my chances, huh?"

Paul ruffled the boy's sweat-soaked hair. No telling how long he'd been up on that ladder, too scared to move a muscle. "It's gonna be fine, you'll see."

"*Jah,* okay. Let's go."

Paul shut the door leading to the silo and breathed a sigh of relief. *Thank You, God, for giving me the courage to climb that ladder and for mending fences between Aaron and me. Might could be he'll finally let me be his friend.*

Barbara put the boys to bed. Hoping to calm her nerves, she was about to fix herself a cup of chamomile tea when the back door swung open. Her heart leaped as Aaron stepped into the room, followed by Paul.

"Thank the Lord, you found him," she cried.

Aaron rushed to his mother's side and wrapped his arms around her waist. "I'm sorry for sayin' such ugly things before and runnin' out of the house thataway. It was wrong, and I know it."

"Your apology is accepted." Barbara leaned down and kissed her son's damp cheek. His eyes were red and puffy, moist with lingering tears. She looked up at Paul. "Where'd you find him?"

Before he could respond, Aaron blurted out, "Way up on the silo ladder. Scared silly, I was, too."

"What?" She gasped. "Oh, Aaron, you know you're not supposed to play in there. It's dangerous. What if you'd fallen? What if—"

"He's okay, Barbara," Paul interrupted. "No harm came to the boy."

Aaron nodded. "Paul climbed up, even though he was scared, and he saved me, Mama. Him and me are gonna be friends from now on." He grinned at Paul. "Ain't that right?"

Paul nodded. "Yep, sure is."

Barbara blinked back sudden tears. This change in Aaron's attitude was an answer to prayer. "I'm so glad, son—about you bein' safe and Paul becomin' your friend." Her gaze went to Paul. *"Danki."*

"You're welcome."

Barbara glanced at Aaron again. "Your hands are dirty. You'd better wash up at the sink."

He did as he was told, and Barbara turned back to Paul. "Would you like to sit a spell and have a cup of tea?"

Paul shook his head. "I appreciate the offer, but I'd better get home. I'm sure there's still some chores needing to be done." He chuckled. "Besides, knowing Mom, she's probably fretting by now. I only told her I was bringing that busted bridle over, so she's most likely wondering what's taken me so long."

"I hope she didn't hold supper on your account."

"Naw, Mom knows if I'm not home when it's time to eat, it means I found someplace else to take my meal."

Barbara smiled as she walked Paul to the door. "Thanks again for rescuing Aaron. Guess I'll see you at church on Sunday."

"You can count on it." He turned and waved at Aaron, who was drying his hands on a towel. "Good-bye, son."

"Bye, Paul."

On the drive home, Paul replayed the events of the evening in his mind. Even though he hadn't been able to tell Barbara what was on his heart, two good things had happened. *I conquered my fear of heights, and I finally made friends with Barbara's oldest son.*

"Now, that's a step in the right direction," Paul murmured into the darkness. Maybe tonight wasn't the time to tell Barbara how he'd come to feel about her. Might be best to wait until he and Aaron had developed a stronger relationship.

Paul clicked his tongue and jiggled the reins to prompt his horse into moving a bit faster. Maybe sticking around Webster County until the harvest was done wouldn't be such a bad thing after all.

twenty-two

"Where have you been so long?" Paul's mom asked when he walked in the door. "Me and your *daed* were gettin' worried."

"Went over to Barbara's to get the bridle fixed and

ended up stayin' for supper," he replied.

"I told your *mamm* that's probably what happened," Pop said with a wink in Paul's direction.

"I'd have been home sooner, but Aaron got stuck on the top rung of the silo ladder and I had to rescue the boy."

Mom's mouth dropped open. "But you're afraid of heights."

Paul shrugged. "I couldn't let the little fellow fall just 'cause I was scared to go up the ladder. But you know, after tonight, I think I could climb up there again and not be afraid."

"I'm glad to hear you've conquered your fear," Mom said.

"Yeah, me, too," Paul responded.

"How are things at the harness shop?" Pop asked.

Paul explained that Samuel Raber's arthritis was acting up again and Barbara was getting further and further behind.

"Harvesting will be done soon," Pop said. "I was wondering if you might consider speaking to Barbara about the possibility of buying into her shop. Sure would make your *mamm* and me glad if you stayed here instead of goin' back to Pennsylvania."

"I'll give the matter some consideration," Paul said. Truth was, he had already come to the conclusion that he wanted to stay in Webster County and work at Zook's Harness Shop. Whether he did that as Barbara's business partner and friend or as her husband remained to be seen.

• • •

Sunday preaching service was held at Samuel Raber's house that week. When church was over and everyone had eaten their noon meal, Paul decided to seek Barbara out and discuss a few ideas he'd been thinking on for the last couple of days.

He didn't see any sign of her on the lawn and figured she was probably inside, either visiting with the women or taking care of the baby.

From his vantage point beside the barn, Paul noticed Aaron across the yard, watching a group of older children playing a game of baseball. It wouldn't be long before the weather would turn cold. Soon the *kinners'* outside games would become snowball fights and sledding.

He pushed his thoughts aside as he approached Barbara's oldest son. "Hey, Aaron, how are you doing?" He clasped the boy's shoulder.

"I wish the older kids would let me play with them."

"Won't be no time a'tall until you'll be included," Paul said. "Why, I think you've grown a couple inches since I first came home in April."

Aaron smiled, and his face turned a little pink "You think so?"

"Sure do." Paul hesitated a moment, then decided to plunge ahead. "Say, I've been thinking—"

Aaron looked up at him expectantly. *"Jah?"*

"I'm planning to go fishing next Saturday afternoon, and I was wondering if your *mamm* might give her permission for you to join me, if you'd like."

"Only you and me? Not Mama and my brothers?"

Paul shook his head. "Just the two of us."

Aaron's lips tuned upward and his dark eyes glistened with obvious anticipation. "I'd like that. *Jah,* I really would."

"Great. I'll speak to your mother as soon as I find her."

The boy pointed to their house. "I think she went inside to feed the *boppli.*"

"Okay, then. Guess I'll just wait 'til she comes outside."

Barbara sat in the rocker and leaned her head back as she fed her hungry babe. She was glad church had been held at her folks' place today. When Davey got fussy, all she had to do was walk a few steps in order to nurse him in the privacy of her own bedroom.

Feeling kind of drowsy, she let her eyes drift shut, enjoying this special time of being alone with her infant son.

Later, as she was putting Davey into his crib, a soft knock sounded on the door.

"Come in," Barbara called.

The door opened and Faith Hertzler stepped into the room. "Is he asleep?" she whispered.

"Jah."

"I wanted to talk, but I guess we'd better do it downstairs so we don't wake the little guy."

Barbara moved over to the bed, took a seat on one end, and patted the spot beside her. "It's okay. Davey's like his *daed*—could sleep through a thunderstorm."

Faith chuckled and sat down.

"What did you want to talk about?" Barbara asked.

"Noah said he was by your shop the other day, and your *daed* mentioned how far behind you're gettin'."

"We've got more work than the two of us can manage, that's for sure."

Faith's blue eyes revealed compassion. "Samuel's arthritis really slows him down, doesn't it?"

Barbara nodded. "I wish I didn't have to rely on Dad's help. But no matter how hard I try, I simply can't do all the work on my own."

"Is Paul plannin' to come back to help after the harvest is over?"

"As far as I know, he'll be returning to Pennsylvania." Barbara swallowed around the lump in her throat. She hated the idea of Paul leaving but didn't know what she could do to stop him from going.

"You're in love with him, aren't you?"

Faith's direct question jarred Barbara dear to her toes.

"Don't try to deny it. It's written all over your face."

Barbara hung her head. "I—I don't want to forget David or let go of what we once had."

Faith draped her arm around Barbara's shoulders. "The scripture tells us in Romans 7:2, 'For the woman which hath an husband is bound by the law to her husband so long as he liveth; but if her husband be dead, she is loosed from the law of her husband.'"

Barbara sniffed as tears formed in her eyes. "I know. But a part of me will always love David."

"And you should," Faith responded tenderly. "He was a wonderful husband and a good father. But he would want you to find love and happiness again, I'm sure of it." She picked up a handkerchief that was lying on the bedside table and handed it to Barbara. "Dry your eyes now and tell me how you feel about Paul Hilty."

Barbara blotted her eyes with the hanky. Then she lifted her head and turned to face her friend. "You're bound and determined to make me say it, aren't you?"

Faith chuckled. "As you may recall, you were pretty determined that I see my need for Noah soon after I returned to Webster County."

Barbara forced a smile. "I knew your place was here, with your family and friends, not on the road tryin' to make a name for yourself. I also knew Noah would make you happy."

"You were right. And I believe Paul can make you happy, as well."

"But I don't know how he feels about me. One minute I think we're getting close, and the next minute he pulls away. It's almost as if he's afraid of something."

Faith patted Barbara's hand. "Maybe he is. Have you asked him?"

Tears hung on Barbara's lashes as a fresh set clouded her vision. "I can't. It wouldn't be right."

"*Humph!* You know how I feel about that notion."

Barbara smiled despite her tears. "I think your time of livin' among the English made you see things in a different light than most in our community."

"When I wasn't following the Lord, I was silly enough to believe the fifth commandment was to humor my father and mother rather than honor them." Faith shook her head. "Only back then, my folks never thought anythin' I said or did was funny."

"That's all changed now."

"Right. Often I'll tell a joke, and my *daed* will laugh so hard he'll have tears runnin' down his cheeks."

"Anything in particular you've told him lately?" Barbara asked, eager for a joke to lighten the mood.

"Oh, sure. I told him the story about the Amish man who went to visit his friend right after a bad storm. 'Did ya lose much in that tornado?' the man asked. His friend replied, 'Lost the henhouse and all my chickens, but that was fine with me, 'cause I ended up with four new cows and somebody's horse and buggy!'"

Barbara laughed. "You sure haven't lost your sense of humor."

Faith smiled but then sobered. "There's one thing I didn't learn while I was livin' in the English world."

"What's that?"

"It's somethin' I grew up knowin' but didn't come to recognize until I moved back to Webster County." Faith moistened her lips. "You need to commit every situation to God. You should be prayin' that the Lord will direct both you and Paul." She squeezed Barbara's fingers. "Keep an open mind and trust in Jesus. If you and Paul are meant to be together, it will all work out."

Barbara drew in a deep breath and released it with a soft groan. "And what of Bishop John? Shouldn't I be praying about his marriage proposal, too?"

Faith frowned and nodded. "*Jah,* you'd better pray about both men."

Barbara opened the front screen door and discovered Paul and Aaron sitting on the porch step. She smiled at the way they had their heads together, talking as though they were the best of friends.

Both of them looked up when Barbara stepped out the door.

"Hey, Mama," Aaron said with a lopsided grin.

"Hey, Aaron. Where are your little brothers?"

"They went for a walk with Grandpa," he answered. "Me and Paul have been sittin' here talkin' about the fishin' trip he wants to take me on this Saturday."

Paul looked kind of sheepish, and his ears turned pink. "I was planning to ask you first, of course," he said, nodding at Barbara.

Barbara glanced at Aaron and couldn't help but notice his hopeful expression. "Would it just be him and you?" she asked, looking back at Paul.

He nodded. "I thought it would give us a chance to get better acquainted."

Barbara stared at the wooden planks beneath her feet as she contemplated the idea. *If he wants to spend more time with Aaron, does that mean Paul has no plans to leave Webster County right away?*

"Can I go, Mama . . . please?"

She smiled. "I think it's a *gut* idea."

"I'd best be going." Paul stood.

Aaron jumped up. "Where to?"

"I've developed a little headache. Think I'll go home and take myself a nap." Paul lumbered down the steps, then looked back over his shoulder. "I'll be by for Aaron on Saturday around one, if that's okay with you."

"One sounds fine."

"And if you have the time, I'd like to discuss something with you then," he added.

"I'll make the time," she replied.

"Okay. See you both on Saturday."

twenty-three

By the end of the week all the hay had been harvested. Paul's dad said he had no problem with Paul taking Saturday afternoon off to go fishing with Aaron Zook. In fact, Paul got the feeling Pop would have liked to go along.

"Sure is a nice day for fishin'," Pop said as Paul hitched the horse to his buggy. "Bet they'll be bitin' real good, too. Won't be long before the weather will be turnin' cold."

"How about you and me going fishing sometime next week?" Paul asked.

"Sounds *gut.* I'll be lookin' forward to it." Pop gave him a nod. "You and Aaron enjoy your day."

Paul grinned and hopped into the open buggy. "I'm sure we will."

Fifteen minutes later, he pulled into the Zooks' yard, eager to take Aaron fishing and anxious to see the boy's *mamm.* Much to Paul's chagrin, he noticed Bishop Frey standing outside the harness shop, talking to Barbara. As far as Paul was concerned, the older man stood much too close to the woman he wanted for his own.

He gritted his teeth and jumped down from the buggy.

Trying not to appear as though he were eavesdropping, Paul stroked his horse behind the ear and strained to hear what the two of them were saying.

"I'm glad you agree," John said with a smile as big as the Missouri River. "I think we'll be very happy together."

Barbara nodded in return. "*Jah,* I hope so."

A knot formed in Paul's stomach, and he nearly doubled over from the pain. Apparently Barbara had decided to accept the bishop's marriage proposal. Paul felt like climbing back into his buggy and heading straight for home, but Aaron came rushing across the yard, waving his fishing pole and grinning from ear to ear. Even though Paul wasn't in the mood to go fishing now, he had promised the boy, so he would see it through. When he brought Aaron home, however, he planned to tell Barbara he was leaving Webster County for good.

She'll probably be glad he thought ruefully. *Then the won't have to worry about me trying to tell her how to run the harness shop.*

With a sigh of resignation, Paul helped Aaron into the buggy, gave a halfhearted wave to Barbara, and pulled out of the yard.

"Sure have been lookin' forward to this day," Aaron said.

Paul nodded. "Me, too."

Paul and Aaron didn't return home until nearly five o'clock. Barbara couldn't wait to hear about their fishing trip and find out what Paul wished to discuss with her. He hadn't said anything before they left, but she'd been busy talking with John Frey. Paul must have decided the matter could wait until after he brought Aaron home.

When Paul halted the horse, Barbara stepped up to the buggy. "Did you two have a good time?"

Aaron jumped down, holding a large plastic sack with a couple of fish tails sticking out. "We each caught two nice catfish, and I almost fell in the pond."

Barbara's gaze went immediately to Paul. "What happened?"

He shrugged. "Aaron was throwing rocks into the water and he slipped. Nearly fell in, but I caught him in the nick of time."

Aaron's dark eyes shone like two shiny pennies. "That's the second time Paul has saved me."

A lump formed in Barbara's throat. It was wonderful

to see Aaron enjoying Paul's company and appreciating him so much.

"Are you two hungry?" she asked.

"I could eat a mule," Aaron exclaimed.

Barbara chuckled. "I'm afraid your grandpa might have somethin' to say if you go after one of his mules." She looked at Paul again. "Would ya like to stay for supper? I've made a big pot of beans and some corn bread."

A shadow crossed Paul's face, and he avoided her gaze. "Thanks anyways, but I'd best be getting on home."

"Aw, can't ya stay awhile?" Aaron whined. "I know my little brothers would like to see you."

"Sorry." Paul leaned over and handed the boy his fishing pole. "Promised my *mamm* I'd be home early tonight, so I'd better be on my way." He gathered up the reins.

"What about the talk we were supposed to have?" Barbara asked. "I thought you had something you wanted to discuss with me."

"It was nothing important. Just wanted to let you know I'll be leaving for Pennsylvania early next week." Paul stared at her a moment. "I hope you have a good life, Barbara."

Before she could respond, Paul lifted his hand in a wave and drove swiftly out of the yard.

"I sure wish he could've stayed to eat with us," Aaron said dejectedly.

Barbara nodded. "Maybe some other time, son."

"But you heard him, Mama. Paul said he'll be leaving soon." Aaron's lower lip trembled, and his eyes filled with tears. "And just when we was becomin' good friends."

Barbara gave Aaron a hug as she fought to control her emotions. "I'm awful sorry, son. Some things aren't meant to be."

Barbara sat straight up in bed. She was drenched with perspiration from having tossed and turned most of the night, dreaming of many things that had put her ill at ease.

She'd seen David in one of her dreams, kissing her good-bye before he headed to town to pick up her anniversary present. John Frey had been in another dream, calmly telling her of his plans for the future. The last dream had Paul Hilty in it, driving away from her house and out of her life forever.

Barbara slipped out of bed and padded across the room to the dresser. She massaged her temples a few seconds, then leaned over the basin. As the cool water hit Barbara's face, she allowed her anxieties to fully surface.

"I've got to sell the harness shop," she moaned. "There's no way I can keep running it on my own." She'd prayed long and hard about this matter and, under the circumstances, felt it was the only thing she could do.

Barbara dried her face on the nearby towel and grimaced. *If Paul leaves Webster County, who will I find to sell the place to? Nobody else in our community does harness work. And without the shop, people will have to go to another town to get their work done.*

Barbara sighed as she glanced at her infant son, sleeping peacefully in his crib. *At least someone in the room isn't feeling the burdens of life this morning.* She moved over to the window and lifted the dark shade. *It has to be Paul who buys the shop. I should have spoken up yesterday when he was here.*

She reflected on Paul's announcement that he'd be leaving sometime this week.

I should have been more prepared for the news. But he has seemed so settled here of late. Ever since he helped Aaron down from the silo, he'd acted like he cared about the boy and wanted to be his friend. *That will never happen if he leaves.*

Barbara paced the room in quick, nervous steps. There was only one thing she could do, and that was to ask him outright not to go. Maybe when Paul heard her offer to sell him the harness shop, he would decide to stay.

"But I'd better move fast," she murmured.

"Where you goin', son?" Paul's mother asked as he started for the back door.

"Thought I'd take a ride. Since I'll be leaving in a few days, I'd kind of like to see the countryside one last time."

Mom frowned. "I still can't get over the announcement you made last night. I don't see why you have to go and leave us again. Don't you know how much your *daed* and I will miss you?"

Paul nodded. "I know, and I'll miss you, too. But with Barbara getting . . ." His voice trailed off. "Oh, never mind." He grasped the doorknob.

"Will you be back in time for the noon meal?"

He shrugged.

"We're havin' Margaret over, along with your brothers and their families." She paused. "And there'll be a couple other guests, as well."

Paul did want to see his sister-in-law again, if just to see how she'd been getting along without Dan. "Okay. I'll try to be back by noon."

"That's *gut,*" she responded. "This might be the last time our family can be together for some time."

"Okay, Mom."

As Paul trudged across the yard toward his buggy, he felt as though he had the whole world sitting on his shoulders. All his plans and dreams had gone out the window in one brief moment when he'd overheard Barbara and the bishop speaking about their upcoming marriage.

The thought had crossed his mind that he could still offer to buy her shop. But being partners wouldn't work. It wouldn't look right for a married woman to be in partnership with a single man who wasn't part of her family. Even if it had been acceptable, he was sure Bishop Frey would put his foot down on that issue.

"I would, too, if Barbara was my wife," Paul muttered under his breath.

Paul stepped into his buggy and grabbed up the reins. Maybe some time alone, with the wind blowing in his face and the smell of crisp autumn leaves tickling his nose, would help calm his anxieties. The buggy ride would also be a good time to do some serious praying.

"Giddyup there, boy," he called to the horse. "You and me have got some riding to do."

twenty-four

Paul had thought the buggy ride would make him feel better, but by the time he returned home, he was even more agitated than when he'd headed out. He didn't want to leave his friends and family again, but he didn't want to stay and see Barbara marry the bishop, either.

In a brief moment of desperation, Paul had considered driving straight to Barbara's and begging her to marry him instead of John Frey. But he'd decided quickly that it was a dumb idea. *She's already chosen him. I'd only make myself look like a fool.* The best thing he could do was to get back to Pennsylvania as quickly as he could and hope he'd be able to forget about Barbara and her boys.

Paul took his time unhitching the horse and putting him in the barn. He dreaded the meal with all his family present. Good-byes would be hard, especially with Mom and Pop so set against him leaving.

When Paul headed around the back of the house,

he was surprised to see Bishop Frey sitting in a chair on the porch. Beside him sat Dan's widow, Margaret.

What's he doing here? Paul fumed.

Gritting his teeth, Paul stepped onto the porch.

"Wie geht's?" the bishop asked.

Paul clenched his fists and forced a smile. "I'm fine, and you?"

"Gut, real *gut."*

Paul looked at Margaret. "You doing okay?"

"Fine and dandy, Paul." She grinned up at him, and he noticed for the first time since Dan's death that Margaret wasn't wearing her black mourning dress. Maybe she'd been counseling with the bishop, and Paul had interrupted. Best he should make a fast exit.

He grabbed the handle on the screen door and was about to open it when Bishop Frey said, "Your *mamm* tells me you're planning to go back to Pennsylvania sometime this week."

Paul gave a curt nod. *"Jah.* I'll probably see about getting a bus ticket tomorrow morning."

"That's too bad," the older man said. "I was hopin' you'd be here for the wedding."

Paul's body became rigid. What was the bishop trying to do—rub salt in his wounds? "I didn't think there was any need for me to see you and Barbara get hitched," he said stiffly.

Margaret gave a little gasp, and John's bushy eyebrows drew together.

"I'm not marryin' Barbara Zook," John said.

Confusion settled around Paul like a thick fog rolling in. "But I thought—"

"It's me John is marrying," Margaret said, her face turning crimson.

Paul felt as if the air had been squeezed right out of his lungs. He grabbed the porch railing to support his knees, which had suddenly gone weak. "When? How?" he stammered.

"We've been seein' each other for a few months now," the bishop replied. "And last week Margaret agreed to become my wife."

"But—but I saw you at Barbara's harness shop yesterday. I overheard you saying—"

"I was telling her about Margaret accepting my proposal."

Paul continued to lean heavily against the rail. If John was going to marry Margaret and not Barbara, that meant Paul still had a chance. At least, he hoped he did.

Drawing in a deep breath, Paul said, "I'm happy for the both of you." He started for the steps. "Would you tell Mom I have an errand to run and won't be able to join the family for lunch after all?"

"She'll surely be disappointed," his sister-in-law said.

He turned to look at Margaret, whose pale blue eyes held a note of concern. "I'll try to be back in time for dessert." Paul hopped off the porch and raced for the barn.

Barbara felt relieved when her mother agreed to watch the boys. Mom was always so good about that, but Barbara didn't want to take advantage of her mother's willingness to help. Mom assured her she enjoyed spending time with the *kinner.* Today, she even said she thought it would do Barbara good to take a buggy ride and be by herself for a while.

As Barbara guided her horse down the lane, she was glad she hadn't told her mother the real reason for this buggy ride. If either of her folks had any idea Barbara was planning to sell the harness shop, they would probably try to talk her out of it. Dad had said many times that he didn't mind helping out, even though he wasn't able to do a lot. He'd told Barbara he knew how important the shop was to her and said he'd do whatever he could to see that it kept running. And Mom, even though she often reprimanded Barbara for working too hard, knew her daughter enjoyed her job and needed to keep working in order to support her family.

Barbara glanced at the darkening sky. "Looks like it could rain," she muttered. She was glad she'd thought to bring an umbrella along. An open buggy offered little protection from the unpredictable fall weather.

She'd only made it halfway to the Hiltys' home when the wind picked up and droplets of water splashed against her face. As she reached for her umbrella under the seat, Barbara spotted another buggy coming from the opposite direction.

Barbara snapped the umbrella open as the buggy approached. She recognized the driver immediately. It was Paul, and from the way his horse trotted down the road, she figured he must be in a hurry to get somewhere.

Barbara slowed the buggy and lifted her hand, waving at him. Paul slowed his rig, too, and motioned for her to pull over to the side of the road.

They stopped under a nearby tree. Paul tied his horse to a sturdy branch, then came around to the passenger side of Barbara's buggy and climbed in.

She scooted over so they could share the umbrella. "The rain sure hit quickly, didn't it?" she asked, feeling suddenly nervous and unsure of herself.

Paul nodded and leaned a bit closer. "I just spoke to Bishop Frey over at my folks' place. He informed me that he plans to marry my sister-in-law, Margaret."

"That's what he told me yesterday afternoon, about the time you were picking Aaron up for the fishing trip."

Paul cleared his throat. "I . . . uh . . . wanted to speak with you then, but after hearing what the bishop said, I figured it was pointless."

"What does the bishop marrying Margaret have to do with your talking to me?"

"I thought it was you he planned to marry. And since I only heard part of your conversation, I got the impression you had agreed to become his wife."

Barbara shook her head. "I told him some time ago that I wouldn't marry him. Unless there's love involved, I couldn't marry any man."

Paul sat there a few seconds, looking perplexed. "I–I totally agree with that, Barbara," he finally said.

"So what did you want to say to me yesterday?"

"I had a business proposition to discuss. But now that I've had time to think it over, I've decided it's not such a good idea."

She tipped her head. "Funny thing. I had a business proposition for you, too."

His eyebrows lifted. "Really? What was it?"

"After much prayer and thought, I've come to the conclusion that I can no longer run the harness shop on my own."

Paul leaned even closer. So close Barbara could feel his warm breath against her face. "Maybe you won't have to," he murmured.

"That's the deduction I came to, as well." Barbara bit her bottom lip, hoping she wouldn't give in to the tears she felt pushing against her eyelids. "I have decided to sell the business, and I was wondering if you might be interested in buying it."

Paul shook his head. "*Nee.* I could never do that. I'd thought I could at one time, but not now."

"Why not? Is it because you prefer living in Pennsylvania?"

Paul lifted Barbara's chin with his finger and stared at her intently. "I'd rather stay here with you and your boys."

She swallowed hard. What was he getting at? "If you want to stay in Webster County, then why not buy my business?"

He inched his head closer. "If I stay, and if I work at the harness shop, it would have to be on one condition."

"What's that?"

"That it be as your husband. I'm in love with you, Barbara."

The shock of Paul's words sent a shiver up Barbara's spine, and she let the umbrella drop to the floor behind them. "Are you askin' me to marry you?"

"*Jah,* if you'll have me."

Barbara thought about the verses of scripture from Ecclesiastes that talked about two being better than one. She drew in a deep breath and released it with a contented sigh. "Oh, Paul, I can hardly believe the way God has answered my prayers."

He raised one eyebrow. "A prayer to keep your shop open, or a prayer to find love again?"

She touched the side of his face and stroked it gently. "Both. But mostly to find love again. I love you, Paul Hilty, but I've been afraid to admit it."

"Why?"

"Because I was scared to open my heart to love again. And I didn't know if you felt the same way toward me."

"Does this put your fears at rest?" Paul's lips sought hers in a kiss so gentle and sweet she felt she could drown in it.

"Oh, yes," she murmured as she stared into his handsome face. "I don't want to be on my own anymore. Two really are better than one. I need someone to share my life with—the joys and the sorrows. I want that someone to be you, Paul."

"Does that mean you'll marry me?"

She kissed the tip of his nose. "I want you to be my life partner as well as my business partner . . . for as long as we live."

epilogue

eighteen months later

"I can hardly believe our first wedding anniversary is next week," Paul said as he cut another piece of leather and handed it to Barbara.

She smiled and leaned over to kiss his bearded face. "Would you mind very much if I give you my gift now?"

"A whole week early?"

"I can't wait a moment longer."

"Sure, go ahead." Paul chuckled and set the leather aside. "Always did have a hard time waiting for things."

She turned to face him, her heart hammering like a stampede of horses. "My gift to you is a son or daughter of your own."

His eyes grew large. "A *boppli?*"

She nodded. "Are you happy about that?"

He wrapped his arms around her. "Oh, *jah,* very happy."

"Does that mean I'm gonna be a big brother again?"

Barbara and Paul turned at the same time. Aaron stood off to one side, his arms folded and a strange look on his face. Barbara hadn't realized he'd come into the harness shop. "That's exactly what it means," she said, praying he wouldn't react negatively.

Paul moved toward the boy. "I hope you know the *boppli* coming won't change anything between you and me, or affect the way I feel about Joseph, Zachary, or Davey."

Aaron grinned up at him. "I know. You've been my new pa for almost a year already, and I won't let nothin' change that—not ever."

Paul gave Aaron a hug, and Barbara joined him. "Now we need to tell our other three sons," she said, blinking against tears of joy.

Paul nodded and bent to kiss her. Even after a year of marriage, the warmth of his lips did strange things to her insides.

"Aw, do ya have to do all that mushy stuff?" Aaron asked, shaking his head.

"You'll be doing the same thing someday, when God brings the right woman into your life." Paul chuckled and boxed the boy playfully on the shoulder. "And if you're really lucky, she'll be able to make Webster County Fried Chicken as good as your *mamm's*."

Aaron grabbed a chunk of leather and headed for the back room. "I ain't never gettin' married," he called over his shoulder.

Barbara smiled at Paul.

He winked, then gave her another hug. "When the

time comes, I hope our boy finds someone as *wunder-baar* as his *mamm*."

She nodded. "*Jah*. No one should spend their whole life on their own. I'm glad I trusted God enough to make the decision to spend the rest of my days with you."

"That goes double for me. Happy anniversary, Barbara Hilty. And may we have many more."

Recipe for Barbara's
Webster County Fried Chicken

1 cut-up frying chicken
1 cup sifted flour
2 teaspoons salt
½ teaspoon pepper
lard

Combine flour, salt, and pepper. Sprinkle additional salt over the chicken. Roll pieces of the chicken in the flour mixture. Melt a few tablespoons of lard in a heavy frying pan. Add the chicken, cover the pan, and fry slowly. Brown the chicken on both sides, then turn the heat to low and continue to cook until the chicken can be easily pierced with a fork.

Center Point Publishing
600 Brooks Road • PO Box 1
Thorndike ME 04986-0001 USA

(207) 568-3717

US & Canada:
1 800 929-9108
www.centerpointlargeprint.com